"What do you think about living at the ranch?" Luc said.

"I like it," Ruby answered.

"Good." Luc captured the little girl in a hug. "Because I like you." He turned back to Cate, waiting for her answer.

"It's not what I expected," she said.

"What did you expect?"

"Actually, I have no idea." She laughed, and Luc smiled.

"Everybody's happy," Ruby said.

"What?" But Cate had an inkling she knew what her daughter meant. Could she tell that her parents were finally getting along?

Luc lowered his voice. "Is she referring to us?"

"I guess she could tell you were making things difficult."

Luc gave an exaggerated snort and then laughed, and Cate's insides warmed like molten chocolate cake. It was nice finding their friendship footing again. Maybe they could get along as parents without letting anything romantic bloom.

The door opened behind her, and Luc's face lit up with recognition. Was it a woman? Scalding jealousy closed off Cate's throat, not boding well for the pep talk she'd just given herself about her and Luc being *just friends*.

Jill Lynn is a member of the American Christian Fiction Writers group and won the ACFW Genesis Contest in 2013. She has a bachelor's degree in communications from Bethel University. A native of Minnesota, Jill now lives in Colorado with her husband and two children. She's an avid reader of happily-ever-afters and a fan of grace, laughter and thrift stores. Connect with her at jill-lynn.com.

Books by Jill Lynn

Love Inspired

Colorado Grooms

The Rancher's Surprise Daughter

Falling for Texas
Her Texas Family
Her Texas Cowboy

The Rancher's Surprise Daughter

Jill Lynn

Recycling programs
for this product may
not exist in your area.

LOVE INSPIRED BOOKS

ISBN-13: 978-1-335-50899-7

The Rancher's Surprise Daughter

Copyright © 2018 by Jill Buteyn

www.Harlequin.com

Printed in U.S.A.

Herein is love, not that we loved God,
but that he loved us, and sent his Son
to be the propitiation for our sins.
—*1 John* 4:10

To my amazing readers, thank you for encouraging me and being a part of this writing journey. Your support means so much to me.

And a huge thank you to Lost Valley Ranch for your help and inspiration.

Chapter One

Nothing like walking into a situation blind.

Lucas Wilder bounded up the lodge steps, the late-July wind that twisted across his sun-scorched arms as dry as aged kindling.

His sister's text that someone was looking for him in the lodge hadn't been helpful in the least. And then she'd gone off radar, not answering his request for more info. Was it an employee? Shouldn't be a ranch guest as last week's were already gone and a new batch didn't arrive until tomorrow.

Luc crossed into the comfortable lobby that guests could relax in after a day of ranch activities, scanning the room for whoever had beckoned as his eyes adjusted to the dim interior lighting.

"Lucas."

The feminine voice slammed into the backs of his knees. He willed his legs not to wobble like a newborn calf's as he faced her.

Catherine Malory. She sat in the club chair stationed to the side of the front window, sunlight streaming over her shoulder, highlighting rich, dark-chocolate hair.

She looked a hint older than the last time he'd seen her. Worried, and yet somehow the addition of a few lines around her eyes and lips only added to her beauty.

Attraction flared to life, the sight of her like oxygen to an ember Luc was certain he'd stomped out years before.

What was she doing here? It had been years since he'd left Denver and their relationship, yet he'd never been able to fully erase Cate from his mind. Luc handled forty-some guests each week plus a slew of employees. Surely he could handle one conversation with a woman he'd once loved.

"Four years." His words quaked out, a cross between teenage boy and wounded animal. Oh, man. He was doing an excellent job of handling it so far.

A crease formed between Cate's slim eyebrows. "I know how long it's been since we've seen each other, Luc. Four years, four months." So like her to have the details exact.

He simply stared, not knowing how long they analyzed each other before he managed to make use of his voice again. "What are you doing here?"

"I—" Her hands clenched together in her lap. "I need to talk to you about something."

Ah. This felt like safe ground. She must need something. Help, he could do. Love? No, ma'am. They'd tried that once. There'd been some immaturity on his part—he could admit that—but mostly he'd loved her, and she hadn't believed him.

"What do you need?" Even after all of

this time, after how they'd left things…he wouldn't turn her away. But hopefully once she said what she needed to, she'd leave. Luc refused to ride that kind of emotional roller coaster again. Since Cate, he'd barely dated. It was easier to focus on work. He had a good life running the guest ranch with his sisters. He was fine on his own. Work might be a lonely companion, but it didn't leave him shattered like Cate had.

"You're going to need to sit down." Her voice came out quiet. Beaten.

"That bad, huh?" Sadness and maybe even a little fear poured from her, and his pulse thundered with curiosity. "Come with me."

When she stood, he led her down the hall to his office for some privacy since a staff member could come through at any moment. Cate shuffled along behind him as though he was directing her to an execution instead of a cushioned seat.

The small space housed a desk, two filing cabinets, framed photos of his family and the ranch in various stages over the years, plus the Top Twenty Guest Ranch Award they'd received the past two years running. Luc motioned for Cate to sit on the charcoal futon that took up one corner.

She sank down, eyes glazed, almost as though she was in shock.

For a moment Luc considered sitting next to her, but the air in the room was already on short supply. Unwilling to risk the close proximity, he perched back against the desk instead, stretching long legs out to hold him steady.

Cate wore a navy shirt with white capris and camel-colored sandals. And even though she looked put together—gorgeous, which he was nowhere near willing to admit— something was definitely off. Luc was almost positive moisture shone in her soft chestnut eyes.

The silence tortured him. "Just tell me, whatever it is." How bad could it be? His mind raced with possibilities. Her parents had been pretty tough on her. Could it be something with them? But what would that have to do with him?

She sucked in a breath, apprehension flitting across her face before she opened her mouth and let loose. "My daughter needs to have surgery." A hand momentarily pressed against her lips as though stemming the flow. "That wasn't how I planned to say that."

"You have a daughter?" Her revelation pierced like a stab wound. Luc would expect that Cate had moved on after him, despite the fact that he'd never accomplished the same himself. But even now, after all of this time, she still felt like his.

But she wasn't. He searched her finger for a wedding ring, but the skin was barren.

Luc shook off the crushing blow. It didn't matter. Their past—her decisions since then—had nothing to do with him. She had a sick daughter. He'd deal with that now. The rest? He'd wait until after she left to process.

"Do you need money?" Where was the father? Why was she coming to him for help?

"No. I need...you."

He had to be missing something. It had been a long time since Cate had needed him. None of this made sense.

"I didn't know until you'd left. I didn't find out until you'd been gone for over a month that I was pregnant, and then I kept waiting for you to contact me, to try to fix things between us. But you didn't."

He resisted a growl. "You told me not to." What she'd said...how she'd said it...he'd never forget it.

"I know what I told you."

His gut bounded for his boots like a loose boulder on a steep hill as he processed the rest of what she'd said. *I didn't find out until you were gone that I was pregnant.*

"Cate." His voice was low and barely existent, but he managed to spit out the question rattling his mind while shock and disbelief ricocheted through him. "What are you saying?"

Remorse brimmed again, and Luc read the truth in the soulful depths before she spoke.

"I'm saying… I'm sorry I didn't tell you sooner. And that she's yours."

Catherine Malory thought she'd understood humility, but she'd never been brought so low as this moment. Who walked into the life of a man she'd lied to, hid a child from for years, and just blurted out that he was a father?

Luc would hate her. And she deserved it. In the beginning she'd felt vindicated keeping Ruby to herself—especially with the way Luc had left and how Cate had grown up being torn between her selfish parents. The feeling of being unimportant had never left her, like a disease that infiltrated her bones.

She'd been attempting to put Ruby first.

To protect her. But Luc would never understand that.

He pushed off from the desk, a long, lean giant in a heather-brown Wilder Ranch T-shirt, faded jeans and boots. "I…have a daughter? You're saying she's *mine*?"

His words ached with a misery that resonated in her own chest. What had she done? "Yes. I'm so sorry. I know an apology isn't enough. I just—"

"Where—" Luc scrubbed a hand through maple hair, though the short cut left little room for mussing. "Where is she?"

"She's here."

His head rolled back as if he'd taken a blow to the jaw.

"We came in, and your sister Emma was headed out to the barn. I remembered her from you talking about her, but of course she didn't know me. She offered to show Ruby the horses after hearing I needed to talk to you. I tried to say no, but Ruby begged to go with her."

And Cate had realized the conversation would be much easier without Ruby present. She hadn't processed through that before she'd gotten in the car and trucked out here. But what would she have done with Ruby anyway? She didn't have family to watch her. A friend would have, but Cate didn't like to be separated from her daughter. Especially with the girl's heart condition.

"Emma's great with kids." Luc's Adam's apple bobbed. "Ru—Ruby will be fine."

Their daughter's name coming from his lips for the first time sent Cate scrambling to keep her careening emotions under control.

"Why are you here now after all of this time? What changed? And how do I know…?" Luc's chest expanded. Cate could imagine his heart beating triple time, because hers felt as though it might explode. His heated hazel eyes held hers. "How do I know she's mine?"

She'd expected it, even planned for it. Still, the sting surprised her. She stated Ruby's birthday at the end of November. Eight months after Luc had hightailed it out of Denver. "When you first left I thought it was stress making me not feel well. Took me a while to figure it out. By then you were long gone."

Every last doubt scrolled across his face.

"Ruby was born with an atrial septal defect."

Luc's hand splayed against his chest where she knew his own scars were. "Same as me."

"As to why now, she needs to have the hole closed. And I couldn't… If something happened to her and you didn't know she'd even existed…" Cate would never have forgiven herself. She already couldn't forgive herself for keeping them apart for the first three years and eight months of Ruby's life.

The familiar rush of fear that came with thinking of Ruby's surgery and anything happening to her precious daughter blurred her vision. "I knew you needed to meet her before her procedure." God had been working on Cate's hard heart, and He'd made that very clear. Almost as though she'd been given a deadline for fessing up.

Since she'd become a Christian about a year ago, Cate had experienced a number of lessons in growing her faith. Trusting God's insistent nudging to tell Luc about Ruby had been the toughest one by far.

Luc scrubbed both hands across his face as though attempting to wake himself from a nightmare.

"We can do a test to prove you're her father. Your name's on her birth certificate."

Arms dropped to his sides like leaded weights. "If you went so far as to do that..." His voice scraped like sandpaper. Worn. Weary. "Why didn't you tell me right away?"

The question she didn't know how to answer. *I didn't want to share* wasn't exactly a mature, adult response.

Luc knew about her childhood—and her parents' divorce—but would he understand how much their actions had messed with her?

"Never mind." The bite in his tone sent guilt skimming across her skin. "It's too late for excuses. Nothing you say is going to matter right now anyway."

"Okay." Cate raised her hands. Whatever he wanted, she'd do.

Luc sank to the other end of the futon, miles of agony stretching between them.

"Does she need open-heart surgery?"

"No. Cardiac catheterization. They'll close the hole with a device."

His shoulders inched lower, his relief evident that Ruby would only need the less invasive procedure that would involve a catheter from her leg into her heart. Already, even with knowing as little as he did about Ruby and possibly not even believing he was her father, he felt for her. Didn't want her to go through the same trauma he had as a child.

That spoke volumes about him.

"Did you tell Emma who the two of you were?"

"No. I think she thought I was a potential

guest or that I was applying for a job." Cate had been purposely evasive.

His audible sigh filled the small space. "That's good. At least for now. Does… Ruby know about me?"

"Lately she's been asking questions, and I've started answering them. She knows you exist, but she doesn't know we're here to see you."

Eyes a mixture of fading green and brown leaves seared into her skin. She half expected to see smoke rise and smell scalded flesh. "In case I didn't see her? If she's my daughter, I would never walk away from her. I think you know that, Cate."

Ouch. That truth stung, as did the *if.* Though she couldn't blame him. Even with Ruby having the same heart defect as he did, why should he believe her? She hadn't exactly proved herself trustworthy over the past four-plus years.

"Do you want to take some time? We can come back. Talk in a few days." If someone had walked into her life and told her news of this magnitude, Cate would be in a puddle on the floor. But not Luc. How was he so calm? Why wasn't he raging at her?

"I'm not sure time is going to change my shock. I want to meet her."

She'd come here for this, but still, her stomach churned. "Are you sure you don't need some time to process?"

He didn't bother to answer. Just raised an eyebrow.

"Okay." If only saying the word out loud would make it true. Cate could tell herself she was okay a million times, but she was afraid the feeling would never follow. "Then let's go."

Luc's boots echoed down the hallway like a death knell on Cate's conscience. Panicked prayers flitted through her mind as she attempted to keep up with his pace. Cate had been praying for Luc and Ruby since she'd figured out this meeting needed to take place, and she could only hope she hadn't ruined either of their lives with her selfishness. Somehow she wanted healing. For all of them.

But today she simply prayed for survival. Good thing she believed in a gracious God. One who forgave her when she didn't deserve His mercy. Because that was the kind of God a girl like her needed.

Luc should probably take some time to process like Cate had suggested, but since nothing made sense right now, he figured, why wait? If he let Cate and Ruby leave, he might never see them again. Cate already seemed so jittery and nervous that he feared losing them both forever. Not that he had them. He wasn't naive. Cate could just as easily disappear from his life again, taking any chance of his knowing Ruby with her. And if she was his daughter, Luc wanted that opportunity.

If she was his daughter. Mind-boggling.

How had his life gone from mundane to unrecognizable in a matter of minutes?

They headed down the lodge steps just as Emma exited the barn, a girl who must be Ruby next to her. The distance allowed Luc to study her. Short little thing—course, she'd only be three years and eight months if Cate was telling the truth. Ruby wore bright pink shorts and a multicolored T-shirt, her animated motions and whatever she said causing Emma to laugh.

After spotting Cate, she ran in their direction, his sister following behind.

Intuitively, Luc had known Ruby would be beautiful—how could she come from Cate and not be?—but the sight of her almost brought him to his knees. Her silky caramel hair was a shade or two lighter than her mother's. Closer to his. He had the niggling sensation that if he rummaged for an old photograph, Ruby would look strikingly similar to his twin sister, Mackenzie, at this same age.

Ruby flung her arms around Cate's legs, and Emma stopped in front of them. "Your girl is a spoonful of honey. We had a good time. Thanks for letting us hang." His sister pulled her hair back and held it at the nape of her neck as a gust of wind wrapped around them.

"Come see me again?" She directed the question to Ruby, who answered with an emphatic nod. After a thank-you from Cate, Emma was off, light brown locks once again twisting in the high-powered breeze as she headed back to the barn. His little sister ran the Kids' Club at the ranch. She was a kid-wrangling, child-whispering rock star.

"Mommy, can we get a horse-y?"

Cate's laugh was strangled. "Our apartment doesn't allow dogs, let alone horses, sweets."

Ruby looked up, noticing him. "Hi." Big brown eyes—just like Cate's—held his.

A rush of emotion clogged his throat, but Luc managed a response. "Hi."

"I'm Ruby. What's your name? Do you live here? Do you have a horse-y?"

Her questions ignited a grin. "Luc." He glanced at Cate, and she shook her head in response to his unspoken question. Ruby must not know his name to be able to create the link to him being her father. Probably a good thing at this point. "And yes, I live here and I have a horse." Or should he say "horse-y"?

He sank to bended knee in front of the girl, partly to be closer to her height, partly because his legs were about to give out.

The blood in his veins thrummed a rhythm that whispered *mine*. As though it knew without a test or proof that Ruby was his daughter.

Why he believed Cate, Luc didn't know. Course, the heart defect seemed a blatant link. When he'd been a child, they hadn't considered it genetic, but in the years since, they'd proved it often was.

Still, he should be careful until he knew for sure.

Yet even with that logical thought backing him up, everything in his body hurt. He wanted so badly to reach out, to hug her, to somehow know everything about her in one instant. He fisted hands at his sides. The idea that Ruby was his, that he'd missed so much time if Cate was telling the truth, made every muscle tense.

"Any chance you want to ride one of the horses?" Everything was better on a horse. Plus, it would give him a chance to get to know Ruby a little.

Her chocolate eyes lit up with excitement, head bobbing fast and furious. She definitely had a sense of adventure. Must drive Cate crazy. The thought warmed him.

"Luc—"

"She'll be fine." He stood, earning crossed arms and a scowl from Cate. Her thin, dark eyebrows joined together in obvious agitation, somehow only managing to highlight her beauty. Luc had never had a problem being attracted to Cate. It was in the mature, getting-along department that they'd struggled.

Luc waited an extra beat to see if Cate added any additional protest. He didn't want to be careless with Ruby, but most often her condition had very few symptoms and just needed to be fixed.

When silence reigned and Cate's shoulders drooped as if relinquishing control, Luc put a check in the victory column. Missing almost four years of Ruby's life definitely gave him an upper hand at the moment.

The three of them headed for the corral, and Luc directed them to Buster, one of the smaller palomino quarter horses with a calm temperament, who was already saddled and ready to go. He hoisted Ruby up and made sure she felt comfortable. Told her where to hold on. Her face shone with wonder and excitement as she commented about how the color of the horse reminded her of caramel popcorn.

"I'm going to walk with you and lead Buster the whole time, and anytime you want to stop or get down, you just tell me."

"I can't do it by myself?"

Adventurous little thing. "Not until you've had more experience. We'd have to get you started on a pony—"

Cate's wide eyes cut him off, communicating all kinds of warning signals and flares. Luc tempered his amusement. He'd probably been getting ahead of himself a bit.

"We'll be back in ten minutes," he said to Cate, lips quirking at her squeak of indignation and the fact that she was, most definitely, not invited.

She'd had Ruby to herself for three-plus years. Luc deserved some time with her away from Cate's hawk-like attention.

Chapter Two

Six agonizing days later Luc paced back and forth near the fireplace in the small living room of his cabin. His friend Gage Frasier perched on the arm of the chair flanking the couch, grilling Luc like the lawyer he was with questions that didn't have satisfying answers.

"Any news on the paternity test?"

"Nope." Luc dropped to the sofa, his body no longer functioning with coherent thought or movement.

He hadn't seen Ruby or Cate since last Saturday because he'd decided the most logical course of action was to wait until he knew for sure that she was his daughter. Though Cate hadn't shown any doubt, she'd agreed to his suggestion that they not say anything to Ruby until they had the paternity test results back.

But waiting was as easy as living with a broken toe.

In the short time he'd spent with Ruby on Saturday while she'd ridden Buster, he'd quickly come to the conclusion that his *possible* daughter was captivating. Entertaining. And bubbled with as much energy as her little body could harness.

The only other time Luc had been smitten so fast was with one other female, who, when he and Ruby had returned to the corral after twenty minutes instead of ten, had been spitting mad.

Luc could admit he had fully enjoyed Cate's disgruntled state. Currently, his guilt meter regarding anything she thought rested solidly at a zero.

Hers should be shooting through the roof. "What's she like?"

"Ruby's..." How to narrow it down? "Sweet. She talks nonstop. The kind of girl who would make friends with a fly." He'd gathered that because she had, in fact, talked to the fly that had ridden on Buster's saddle horn for part of the ride. And she'd befriended Luc instantly, jabbering the whole time. He'd learned that she had a best friend at day care and that her mom didn't let her do more than an hour of "lectonics" in a day even though some kids got to do bunches more.

That one had made him smile. He'd found himself silently agreeing with Cate.

Ruby had told him her mom read "lots" of books to her every night, announcing it as though she was the most special girl in the world and their reading time only confirmed it.

That information had created an uncomfortable surge of sympathy in Luc, flooding him with images of Cate juggling everything on her own. Ruby and her condition. Work. Bills. How had she managed it all? From what he knew of her parents, he couldn't imagine them stepping in to help when Cate had found out she was pregnant. But he'd quickly stomped out the rush of concern that came with imagining Cate doing everything on her own.

He was *not* going to feel bad for her. Not after the decision she'd made to keep Ruby from him.

Luc had gotten a DNA test done in town first thing Monday morning. They'd sent in his sample, and Cate and Ruby had gone to the testing place in Denver. Now it was ticking toward five on Friday, and he was tormented to think he'd spend the weekend without knowing the results. So much felt undecided. And on top of his questions, Cate had texted him the date of Ruby's procedure. One week from today.

"So Cate didn't explain why she never told

you about Ruby?" Gage's dark hair looked as rumpled as Luc's. At least he could count on sympathy and understanding from his friend. Gage had been through a horrible ordeal when his wife left. Sometimes Luc wondered if the man would ever recover.

"Nope. But I really didn't let her. What does it matter? What's done is done." Anger boiled under the surface. Those last two comments were lies. He both wanted to know what Cate had been thinking and felt so wounded and aggravated that he didn't believe any answer she gave would help.

"Luc." Gage's voice snapped with concern, but Luc wasn't sure he could handle any more girl talk—problems that didn't have solutions were his least favorite subject. "Your phone just buzzed." Gage motioned to the coffee table.

Luc snagged it and opened the new email, relief tingling through his limbs when he saw it contained the results. Sawdust coated his mouth, saliva running for the hills. He clicked to read the report, the letters swimming before him. *Not Excluded* was typed across the top of the page in bold print. The testing facility had coached him on what this meant.

He was Ruby's father.

The phone slipped from his grip, bouncing lightly on the sofa cushion.

"I'm a dad."

It was as though he'd taken a horse kick to the chest, the air in his lungs instantly gone. He and Gage stared at each other. Frozen.

Unable to stay still, Luc pushed up from the couch, his strides quickly covering the small cabin's living room. He ended up at the back window that faced open ranchland, seeing the grass-covered hills in a new light. Yesterday it had been land passed down to Luc and his sisters when their parents had moved to a warmer climate in order to accommodate his mom's health. Today a new generation existed. A little girl with silky hair and a nonstop mouth and adorable brown eyes who was his. *His.*

"I have to see her." He crossed the space and rummaged for his keys in the kitchen junk drawer.

Gage followed him. "Don't you think you should wait? Calm down first?"

Why did he have so many scraps of paper in this stupid drawer? Items tumbled over each other as he searched for the simple metal key ring. "I don't see a real possibility of that happening in the very near future."

"Guess not." Gage nudged Luc to the side, then found the truck keys in a much calmer, more methodical manner.

But then again, Gage hadn't just found out he was positively a father.

His friend offered up the keys on the palm of his hand. "Do you want me to go with you?"

Luc appreciated Gage's support, but he needed some time to clear his head. Maybe the drive would help, though he wasn't confident anything would at the moment. "Nah. Thanks, though." He snatched the metal ring that held three keys and proceeded to the front door, snagging his boots.

"What are you going to do? About custody?"

He paused to glance at Gage after yanking on the first boot. "What do you mean? What can I do?"

"File for it."

"I don't know." He couldn't think beyond seeing Ruby right now. Couldn't deal with logistics. "I'm angry, but I'm not sure that's the answer."

"You need to protect yourself. She's already kept Ruby from you for years. Who's to say she won't take off and disappear to another state and you'll never see your child again?"

Red flashed, and Luc pulled on the second boot with heated force. Cate wouldn't... would she? But the same thought had entered his mind. When they'd readied to leave on Saturday, Luc had wondered if he'd ever see them again. Cate had written down her address and phone number, almost as though proving to him she wouldn't do anything of the sort.

Still, how could he trust her after what she'd done?

"Do you want me to look into it? See what your options are? I know someone who deals with these situations. I can ask."

Gage was the only man Luc knew who ranched as a later-in-life choice. He'd been a smarty lawyer at some big firm until he'd inherited a ranch from his uncle. Gage and his wife, Nicole, had moved to the nearby ranch just over a year and a half ago. And then Nicole had decided a different life looked better, and she'd been gone in a blink. Gage had been on his own ever since. He ran the ranch, very quietly helping the church or people in the community out with legal matters when they required it.

Luc just never imagined he'd be in need of that advice.

"I don't know that I have any other choice." A stampede of hooves vibrated inside his skull. "I'm not sure if I have any rights and if she can control letting me see Ruby. So, yeah. Check it out."

"I will."

"Good thing I have you on retainer."

Gage chuckled. "You don't. You couldn't afford me. This friend business really works in your favor."

"True."

Luc grabbed the piece of paper with Cate's address from the kitchen counter. He'd left it there as a reminder to pray for Ruby—not that the trigger had been necessary. The girl and her mother hadn't left his thoughts all week.

He'd need the details if he planned to show up on Cate's doorstep unannounced.

It wasn't very considerate of him to plan to ambush her at their home. But then again, he hadn't expected Cate to show up on his doorstep with a daughter he never knew he had.

Turnabout was fair play.

"Mommy, will you play the cupcake game with me?" Ruby stood before Cate with a well-loved game in her hand that still boasted the reduced thrift-store sticker price.

Before Ruby, Cate had never stepped foot in a secondhand store. She'd never struggled for money growing up. But love and attention? Those had been harder to find.

It wasn't as if her parents had been abusive in any way. She'd just been more…overlooked. They were simply too caught up in themselves to notice anyone around them— including the little girl left in the wake of their selfishness.

Growing up, her parents never saw eye to eye on anything, but on the subject of her pregnancy, they'd instantly been in agreement. They'd advised her that having Ruby would ruin her life. That it would be too hard. That it would crumple any chance of her being successful and she'd have to scramble to make ends meet. They'd told Cate that if she kept the baby, there'd be no help from them. Money or otherwise. Probably hoping to sway her decision. It hadn't worked. But it had left them estranged.

They'd been right. Cate had hustled. Finished school early on an accelerated path. She'd scrounged for work, taking anything and everything she could find. Raising Ruby was the hardest thing she'd ever done in her life.

But her parents had also been so very, very wrong. Because the adorable munchkin standing in front of Cate hopping up and down—game pieces rattling inside the box as though agreeing with her impatience—was by far the best thing she'd ever accomplished. Worth every second of her energy and love.

"Please, Mommy?"

"Okay, Rubes. I'll play." After a couple of games Ruby would have a little more play-time and then Cate would read to her before bed. She still went down early—partly for Cate's sanity and partly because she often worked the evening hours until falling into bed herself.

Removing the charcoal-framed glasses she wore for computer work, Cate set them next to her Mac computer on the desk that occu-pied one corner of the living room in their tiny, two-bedroom apartment.

The screen in front of her went dark as it fell asleep, but she knew what lurked behind the curtain of black. A project with a loom-ing deadline. She was close, but she couldn't quite get the branding package for the local cupcake shop just right. And she needed it to be perfect, because she needed the next freelance job after this. Cate loved her ca-reer as a graphic designer and the freedom it allowed her to work from home and cart

Ruby to and from the small in-home day care she went to.

A majority of Cate's jobs came from a firm in Denver who hired her as a subcontractor, and she filled in the extra income they needed with side work.

They moved over to the sofa, and Ruby set up the game while Cate covered a yawn and considered making a cup of tea. Twenty-four years old and this was what she'd come to on a Friday night. But then, getting pregnant at twenty had put a damper on any wild and adventurous life plans.

Ruby chose a blue base and began building a cupcake. She never really followed the game cards, instead creating whatever combination suited her fancy at the moment.

"Your turn, Mommy."

Cate picked the yellow holder, choosing to add a plastic layer of chocolate, wishing, not for the first time, that this game consisted of real cupcakes and she could inhale the chocolate one in her hand…after adding a layer of buttercream frosting.

Her mouth watered just as a knock sounded at their door, causing her to jump like a popcorn kernel in sizzling oil.

Who would be at their door on a Friday night? Was it her nosy neighbor again? Millie Hintz wasn't the landlord, but she'd appointed herself as the head of the building's nonexistent neighborhood watch program. A spry eighty-year-old with white hair who seemed to be shrinking in height over time, her unexpected pop-overs were unnerving because she always scanned the apartment from the doorway like she was going to catch Cate with a hidden mountain lion or other unapproved item.

But even though Millie considered it her job to know what was happening in everyone's lives, she was kindhearted. Cate had decided the visits were more about loneliness than anything else. And if anyone understood that, it was her. Talking to Millie wouldn't cost her more than a few minutes of time.

"You go," she told Ruby, pushing up from the sofa and crossing the few steps to the door. Sometimes Millie brought them cookies. The monster ones with M&M's and chocolate chips. Yum.

Cate pressed her face against the peephole, squeaking in surprise when it wasn't shrinking Millie on the other side of the door, but Luc.

What was he doing here?

All week he'd been on her mind, her thoughts zipping into overdrive… Had she done the right thing telling him about Ruby? She hoped so. It had taken all of her strength to share her daughter with him. They'd done the DNA testing earlier this week, and she'd let him know about Ruby's procedure date, but other than that, she hadn't heard from him. What was he thinking showing up at their apartment like this? Didn't the man know how to use a phone?

And more important, did he know she was home and did she have to answer? Her pulse bumped along like her car had on the gravel road that led to the Wilder ranch. And of course she was in old, black, faded-to-gray yoga pants and a yellow V-neck T-shirt, her hair in a disheveled low ponytail.

Quite the package.

Frustration leaked out in a disgruntled huff. "So much for cookies." She'd take Millie over Luc any day.

"I can hear you through the door, Cate."

She jumped to the side as if he had X-ray vision and could also see her through the barrier.

"You really know how to creep a girl out." Cate quickly redid the tie that held her hair and swiped under her eyes for runaway makeup.

"Are you going to open the door or are we going to keep talking through it?"

Ruby appeared next to Cate. "Is that my friend Luc?"

Ever since they'd been to the ranch, Ruby hadn't stopped chattering about "my friend Luc." It was all Cate could do to keep from plugging her ears, because she didn't have a clue what was going on in Luc's head since she'd shown up and royally flipped his life upside down.

She both wanted and didn't want to know what he was thinking.

What he thought of her.

"Yep, it is." Cate undid two locks with shaking fingers—not that the security mattered so much now that she knew how flimsy her door was—and twisted the knob.

Luc practically took up the whole frame. What was it about him that always made her feel like his presence sucked the oxygen out of the room? He wasn't *that* tall. Maybe an inch under six foot.

His eyebrow quirked. "Can I come in?"

Was answering *no* a legitimate option? Ruby nudged past Cate, latched on to Luc's hand and pulled him inside. The scent of the outdoors came with him.

"Come on. I want to show you my room and my new doll and my ponies and my pink lamp. Me and Mommy were playing a game. You can play with us if you want."

The adoration for Ruby written on Luc's face was enough to make Cate's knees go swirly. Though none of it was directed at her.

An annoyed *meow* sounded from the top of the couch. Princess Prim rose from her favorite resting place and stretched her spine as if their ruckus had woken her and she was *not* pleased about it. Narrowed eyes dissected Luc, naming him an intruder in one fell swoop. *Good kitty.* Cate silently promised her a treat for later.

"I thought you couldn't have pets." Luc's head swung from the feline to Cate.

"We can't have dogs, but Prim is more royalty than pet. She runs the place. Ruby and I are just her lowly servants."

Ruby giggled and gave Luc's hand—which she hadn't let go of—a determined tug. She yanked him across the small apartment living room and past their dining table. But at the threshold to her bedroom, Luc paused.

"You okay if she shows me her room?"

A dried biscuit had somehow gotten lodged in her throat. Considerate of him to ask, but Luc had as much of a right to Ruby as she did.

That was what scared her the most.

Cate managed a nod, and the two of them disappeared inside. She heard Ruby's continuous chatter and Luc's low voice rumbling back questions or answers. The whole thing made her drop to the couch and hold her head in her hands. What had she done?

God, You'd better be right. Protect her. And me. Please. You know I didn't want to do this.

Princess Prim burrowed onto her lap, tilting her head in a way that asked questions. The royalty wanted answers Cate didn't have.

"What are you? The press?" She scrubbed hands into the soft fur behind Prim's ears. "I just don't want her to get hurt. And I'm afraid of losing her." The whisper came out forlorn, and Prim purred in sympathetic response.

What were the two of them doing in there? Moving Prim to the sofa, Cate eased to the edge of Ruby's room, close enough to hear but not be seen.

Prim let out an incriminating meow. She'd followed Cate and now rubbed against her leg. Cate nudged her gently away with her foot and put her finger to her lips in a shushing motion—as if the cat could understand her. The move only caused Prim to meow with interest and sneak between her feet as though they were playing a game. Cate's hiding place wouldn't last long at this rate.

Tea. She could make that cup she'd been craving earlier. It wasn't eavesdropping if the kitchen happened to be almost directly across from Ruby's doorway.

Cate made her way toward the pint-size kitchen as slowly as possible, her lungs constricting at the sound of Luc's booming laughter mingling with Ruby's sweet giggle. She caught sight of Luc perched on the bed and Ruby on the floor, her head bent in concentration as she showed him something.

And then, instead of finding herself in the kitchen, she was standing in the doorway. Both of them looked up as if questioning the reason for her presence.

"Hey, I..." ...*wanted to hear what you were saying.* "Does anyone want something to drink? Luc? I didn't even offer." *When you showed up unannounced at my door.*

Good thing none of these snarky thoughts were actually coming out of her mouth.

"I'm fine, thanks," Luc answered, and Ruby shook her head.

Dismissed without a second thought. Eerily similar to her childhood. The emotion wrapped around Cate like an old, tattered blanket she'd tried to throw out more times than she could count. But somehow every time she opened her closet, there it was.

Cate microwaved water in her favorite Anthropologie monogram mug—a fabulous thrift-store find. At the insistent beeping that the microwave had finished its work, she popped open the door and dunked her finger into the liquid to check the temperature.

Ouch. She snatched her poor skin back out. Scalding.

Ripping open the calming tea bag—like it would make a dent in her current state of mind—Cate bobbed the trapped tea leaves in the cup, her agitation sending ripples across the water.

When she'd first found out she was pregnant with Ruby, Cate had felt vindicated in not contacting Lucas. He'd never tried to fix what had gone wrong between them or answer the accusations she'd questioned him about in the end. Yes, she'd confronted him about cheating on her after a friend had tipped her off. But Cate had just wanted answers. Wanted Luc to tell her he wasn't seeing someone else and confirm the truth she already felt in her bones. He had quickly denied doing anything of the sort…but the more she'd pushed for details, the more he'd shut down.

They'd fought and said so many horrible things to each other.

Cate sipped her tea, leaning back against the countertop, eyes closed against the memory of that night as hot liquid coated her throat. Man, they'd been young. Stubborn. And completely inconsiderate of each other.

Finally, she'd told him to leave. To never contact her again.

The strangest part was, he'd listened. Cate didn't plan to tell the man currently one room away from her that she'd waited for him to fight for her. To love her. She'd wanted to have a calm conversation about what happened—to find out the truth and listen to Luc—not just lob accusations back and forth.

But she hadn't heard from him after that night. Only radio silence.

Cate crumpled the tea package while blinking away unwanted moisture. She tossed it into the garbage and slammed the cupboard door shut. But the askew trash can blocked it from closing, not giving her the pleasure of a loud crash.

She attempted to leave it for all of two seconds, then groaned and opened the door, straightening the wastebasket so that the cabinet shut flush.

After Ruby had been born and the heart defect had been found, Cate had been so focused on her daughter that she'd attempted to put Luc out of her mind.

She'd decided she was right to keep Ruby to herself. That she was protecting her daughter from being subjected to parents who didn't get along—Cate knew too well the kind of wounding that could inflict on a child. Even after they'd grown into an adult.

She'd clung to bitterness and fear, letting them dictate her choices.

Until just over a year ago. Through a little girl and her mom at day care who invited Ruby to attend Sunday school, Cate had found herself on a padded church chair for the first time in her life. She'd met God within those walls, and a piece of her that had always felt forgotten became known.

God had worked on her over the year, slowly convincing her that while she might not be able to trust Luc or even herself, she could trust Him. Ruby needing the procedure had been the last key in getting Cate to tell Lucas the truth.

But she was still afraid.

That Luc would try to take Ruby away from her. That his presence would wreak havoc on the safe life she'd so carefully woven for them. That she'd foolishly be drawn to him all over again.

If Luc decided to be a part of Ruby's life, Cate's focus would remain on their daughter.

She wasn't going to entertain any attraction to Luc or let her mind wander regarding how things had gone wrong so quickly between them at the end.

Cate refused to leave a shattered little girl in the wake of any of her own selfish desires.

Which led to the main question throbbing behind her temples with ferocity. Did she even need to worry about Luc being in their lives? Why was he here tonight? Was it to tell her he was in?

Or out?

Chapter Three

The scent of garlic in Cate and Ruby's apartment—a remnant of dinner, Luc would guess—made his stomach growl. In his hurry to get here and see Ruby, he'd forgotten to eat. Not a normal occurrence for him.

He sat on Ruby's bright purple bedspread while she showed him her colorful ponies. He'd already met her collection of dolls.

On his way into Ruby's room, Luc had given the apartment a quick once-over. The size of a matchbox with everything in its place. So Cate was still the neat freak she'd once been. But the pieces and colors she used in the apartment gave it a comfortable feel. Artistic and homey. Even still, Luc felt strangely claustrophobic. He was used to wide open spaces. The building barely had any grass outside with no playground to be seen.

He had the strangest urge to snap Ruby into his arms, barrel out of here and never come back.

"This one's my favorite." Ruby held up a white pony with purple hair.

At times she talked so fast Luc could barely decipher her words. For the most part he'd been drinking her in—watching the nuances that made her unique—while trying not to overdo it with his interest. So far he'd learned she tugged on her earlobe when she was thinking and that she rarely stayed in one position for more than sixty seconds.

See? She needed a ranch for a backyard. But that wasn't Luc's focus in being here. It was to discuss the paternity test results with Cate, and then for the two of them to tell Ruby he was her father. He needed to stay on point.

"It's time to get ready for bed, Rubes." Cate stood in the doorway to the room, her bare toes peeking inside.

Luc glanced at the small clock on Ruby's nightstand, surprised to see how much time had passed since he'd arrived.

"But…" Ruby's brow pinched, her voice escalating to a whine. "But my friend Luc is here."

Her friend Luc. Sweet girl. Little did she know how her life was about to change. Luc prayed it would be for the better and that she'd adjust without the news harming her or causing turmoil.

"I know," Cate answered with patience and a hint of weariness, "but it's getting late and you need your sleep. We can still read a story if you get your pajamas on and brush your teeth." She infused pep into the last part, but it was lost on Ruby.

A storm of opposition continued to brew in

the half-pint in front of him. Luc pushed up from the twin bed, the frame creaking under his added weight. "I need to talk to your mom. I'll do that while you get ready and then maybe..." He looked to Cate. "Maybe I can read you a book?"

After a moment of hesitancy evidenced by the thumbnail slipping between Cate's teeth, she nodded.

Luc followed Cate out of the room, shutting the door behind him and stopping in the middle of the living room. If he walked out the space from wall to wall, he'd probably only get in six long strides. Had it shrunk even more while he was with Ruby? Or maybe it was just being near Cate with no daughter as a buffer.

"I got the test results back. Ruby's mine." His throat tightened. How had they gotten here? Anger and confusion and sadness all whipped through him like a gust of Colorado wind. "They sent an email a little bit ago."

No surprise showed on Cate's features at

his announcement. But then, he hadn't accused her of cheating on him four years ago. The opposite had happened. And it had been the worst moment of his life when he'd denied doing any such thing…and she hadn't believed him.

Luc couldn't stand it when someone didn't trust him. He'd lived that back in high school and then again with Cate, and he had no desire to repeat the scenario.

Cate motioned to her computer. "I haven't checked my email, so I didn't get it yet, but I also don't need it. I know she's yours." Weighty silence stretched between them. "But I'm glad you have the answers you need."

"So now what?"

"I don't know." Her hands lifted, their slight shaking gunning for his sympathetic side. He quickly slammed the door on that unwarranted response. "I guess that's up to you. How involved you want to be. If you want to see Ruby."

"If?" Heat seared his voice. Was she joking? Didn't she know him better than that? Cate looked as though she was about to dissolve into an emotional flood, and despite his outrage, Luc didn't want that. Especially for Ruby's sake. They didn't need to start out back in the same boxing ring they'd ended in the last time. He made a second attempt to answer her in a calmer tone. "Of course I want to see her."

"Then I guess we figure out a plan. A schedule."

Luc wanted all of Ruby in his life, not a color-coded calendar of planned times. But that was impossible. Even if he did want to transport Ruby out of this place, he couldn't. Cate would never stand for it. He wasn't that much of a fool.

"What about telling her?"

Her eyes momentarily closed, fingertips massaging her temples. "I've been prepping her as much as I could. I asked her if she'd want to meet her father."

"What did she say?"

Ruby scampered into the hallway. "I'm gonna brush my teeth, and then I know what book I want my friend Luc to read. Boo-boo bear picked it out. But, Mommy, I still need you to huggle me."

After that barrage of information, the bathroom door banged shut.

Luc needed a three-year-old translator. "Huggle?"

"Snuggle and hug combined." Cate's face softened, the curved lips that surfaced over Ruby enough to take out a man with less resentment propping him up at the knees. "And in answer to your question, you've met her—what do you think she said? To Ruby, the more, the merrier. She wants to meet her dad. You."

"So we'll tell her tonight?"

The enormousness of his question made filling his lungs an impossible task. It must have affected Cate the same, because her chest stuttered numerous times as it rose and fell.

"Yes." Sorrow lines surrounded liquid brown pools of remorse. "Luc, I really am sorry."

And he really didn't want to hear it right now. One day they'd have to get into the whys. One day he'd have to move toward forgiving her. Today was not that day.

Luc had been talking to God plenty about Ruby and Cate this week, reaching for answers that felt miles away. And while he knew the man upstairs would be nudging him to deal with his ire toward Cate in no time at all, tonight was about telling Ruby the truth.

When he didn't answer her apology, Cate sucked in a breath too big for her small frame, as if gathering courage. "I need—" her eyes found his and held, pleading "—to know you're in. Not with me—I get that I'm not high on your list of favorites right now. But for Ruby's sake, I need to know you're not just going to cut and run when you figure out being a dad is the hardest thing you'll ever do. I have to know she can count on you."

Despite all the wrong that had transpired between them, Cate was right to ask. To protect her daughter—*their* daughter. A smidgen of respect eased back into play. "I don't do anything halfway, Cate. So in answer to your question, I'm not going anywhere. I'm in Ruby's life for good."

Though Luc didn't know how they were going to tell Ruby. How to explain why he hadn't known about her without making Cate look bad. Because no matter what tension ebbed between him and Cate, he wouldn't start out by maligning Ruby's mother. He *would* put their daughter's needs first.

Luc silently fired off prayers for guidance and wisdom.

Cate's eyebrows plunked together like magnets. "What are you thinking?"

"I'm praying." The answer snapped out a

little snarly—ironic, considering the statement. Again, Luc dug for civility. "I've never done this before. I don't have a clue what I'm doing. What we're supposed to do now." He shrugged, offering an olive branch. "So I thought I'd ask someone who does."

Disbelief and curiosity warred on her face. "Since when are you a praying man, Lucas Wilder?"

"Since I left…" *You.* "…Denver. Once I moved back to the ranch, I was…" *A mess.* "I started going to church with my family and it was like something clicked. I'd never really wanted a relationship with God when I was younger, but something changed. And so did I." At least he hoped he had. Luc sure hadn't handled things well with Cate back when they'd been together. He'd done a lot of putting himself first. Had he appreciated Cate back then? Doubtful.

His immaturity during their relationship— including the fact that they'd been pretending to be adults when they were anything but—smarted like a hoof to the shin.

"Ruby and I...we go to church, too. I became a Christian about a year ago." A begrudging tilt claimed her lips. "It's the reason you're standing here right now. Otherwise, I'm not sure I would ever have softened." She shrugged, one shoulder lifting the messy ponytail that had loosened to cascade down her back.

Seeing Cate so casual tonight—without the armor of her well-put-together clothes and wearing very little makeup—made Luc flash back to their younger days. She'd been beautiful back then, but now there was something about her... Maybe it was peacefulness. He wasn't sure. But he liked this casual side of her. Cate looked ready to snuggle up on the couch with a blanket and watch a movie. And the traitor side of him thought he should be the one tucked in next to her. She had that effect on him, and he was still furious with her.

What would happen if he actually managed to forgive Cate? Maybe that was part of the reason he didn't want to—because Luc refused to go anywhere near the possibility for that kind of anguish again.

The kind they'd caused each other.

In all of his aggravation at Cate over the past week, Luc had conveniently forgotten one thing...his fault in what had happened. What he'd been like back then. Even before their last fight, he'd often been quick to tussle with her over the smallest things. They'd been so young, their relationship on fast-forward.

Luc had thought he loved Cate then...but now he wondered if he'd ever truly understood the definition of the word.

Since Cate had reappeared in his life, he'd been so focused on the mistakes she'd made in keeping Ruby from him that he hadn't even considered his selfish decisions.

"I was a jerk when we were younger, wasn't I?"

Cate had the grace not to answer him, but Luc knew the truth.

No wonder she hadn't told him about Ruby. If it had been him in her shoes, he wouldn't have contacted himself, either.

Cate had been in too many hard, unforgiving chairs in doctors' offices like the one currently holding her, but today something was different. Luc occupied the seat next to her.

Ruby climbed all over him, the heat from his lanky frame seeping into Cate's personal space. Of course, he hadn't lost his temper once dealing with all of Ruby's pent-up energy while they waited. But then, he'd only been acting as a parent for six days. He'd fail soon enough, and then she'd feel guilty for entertaining this thought process at all.

Cate had read enough about Ruby's condition to know that not every office did nurse consultations before the procedure, but she was thankful theirs did. The more information she had, the better.

"Do they normally run behind?" Luc asked.

"Not too bad. If you have somewhere you need to be, you can go."

His eyes narrowed at her sugar-sweet offer. "Trying to get rid of me?"

Yes. "No."

The grin commandeering his mouth said he knew exactly what she was thinking and doing. Attraction came unbidden, a surprising shimmy in her gut. *Down, girl. Not your candy.*

He leaned closer, and her body sent off warning flares. Jump ship advisories blared. "I already told you that I'm here for Ruby no matter what. That I want to be a part of her life. The question is whether you're going to let me be."

Since when had Luc turned into this wiser, calmer version of the barely adult man she'd once known?

In the living room the other night, before they'd talked to Ruby, he'd even prayed with her. They'd stood three feet apart and been separated by miles of unresolved issues, but the prayer had held more intimacy than she'd expected.

Luc had asked God to show them what to say and what not to say and to give Ruby an open mind.

The prayer had worked.

When they'd told Ruby that Luc was her dad, she'd asked a few questions that they'd done their best to answer, but for the most part, she'd been more focused on the future than the past. Though Cate imagined those tougher questions would come with time and age, and it would be her job to do the explaining.

Then Ruby had asked if she was going to see Luc again.

Cate had pondered the same question many times as she'd contemplated telling Luc about Ruby.

In answer, Luc had held Ruby's hand in his oversize one. He'd told her he would *always* be in her life—that they were a part of each other—and nothing would separate them again. Ruby had listened intently. The next day she'd started referring to him as "my dad" instead of "my friend Luc."

After Luc had gone back to the ranch that night, Ruby had been unable to sleep from her excitement. She'd told Cate all of the things she wanted to do now that she finally had her own dad. As if she'd gone into a store and picked one out from the shelf.

Camping. Fishing. Where had Ruby come up with those ideas? Probably from a kiddo at day care. Riding a horse again. Cate wasn't sure whether to be relieved or irritated at Ruby's immediate acceptance of Luc.

Of course, she *should* feel the first. But the second was just so within reach. All of a sudden, their lives were flipped upside down—like a bug on its back, legs wiggling to find traction in thin air. Ruby felt okay with that, obviously, but Cate didn't. She wanted safety back. She wanted to be the only one at this visit instead of one half of a parenting duo.

Cate was definitely having a hard time letting Luc into their lives. And the worst part was, he knew it. He knew her too well. She'd made plenty of changes in the years since they'd dated, but there was still a little girl living inside her who struggled with rejection and trust.

Who couldn't forget the lessons her parents had taught her.

She'd been ten when her parents divorced. Some couples fought for custody because one parent was unstable or unsafe. Because they believed a certain home was the better place for their children.

But hers had simply fought to fight. It hadn't been about protecting her, but more that they didn't want to give in to each other. She'd been collateral damage in their war.

A lost girl who knew intrinsically she wasn't significant in the grand scheme of their relationship or divorce.

Cate didn't want that for Ruby. It was part of why she hadn't told Luc about her. Cate was afraid of losing her daughter. Fearful that Luc would fight for custody and then Cate would be just like her parents—focused on a battle instead of on Ruby.

She wanted Ruby to always feel important. Loved beyond a shadow of a doubt. To never experience the tumultuous pieces of childhood Cate had.

Not that Cate could tell Luc all of that. He would never understand why she'd kept Ruby from him. No answer would be good enough, and she had to be okay with that. Just like she had to figure out how to be more Ruby-like about him being in their lives.

The door to the room opened, and the nurse came in. Diane. They'd had her many times before. She slid a wheeled stool up to

Ruby while greeting them, and Cate introduced her to Luc.

"Ruby." Diane held a teddy bear, one that had obviously been used numerous times as an example. "In two days Dr. Thom is going to fix a small hole in your heart, just like fixing Mr. Bear's tear right here." She motioned to the small gap in the brown fur. "You won't feel it. You're going to fall asleep like Sleeping Beauty, take a little nap, and when you wake up it will be all better."

Ruby listened, enraptured by the idea of starring in her own fairy tale. "Okay, Dr. Thom fix it." She went back to playing with the supplies from her activities bag—a small board she could draw on and then erase.

Over the years and appointments, Cate had told Ruby she had an extra-special heart that held lots of love and needed checkup appointments. She'd accepted that news just as easily as this. Of course, she was too young to truly understand the concept of surgery, but they did need to at least give her an idea of what was to come.

Dr. Thom's whole staff was exceptional about knowing what to say and how to say it to make little minds understand.

Now, if only they had something to eliminate Cate's apprehensions.

Cate let Ruby wear headphones and watch a movie on the iPad while Diane outlined the procedure for her and Luc. Diane talked through a few pages of information, including some visuals, then asked if they had any concerns.

"What will her recovery be like?" For some reason Luc's question surprised Cate, but then, he had the right to be involved. He was here, wasn't he? She should be thankful that he was committed to Ruby—that her daughter could depend on him—instead of being so panicked by what his presence meant.

Pull yourself together, Cate. Even if you can't trust him, you can trust God. The mantra that had gotten her to the Wilder ranch in the first place eased a smidgen of uneasiness.

"With cardiac catheterization, the recovery is minimal," Diane answered. "Nothing like open-heart surgery. Rest is needed while the incision site heals, but many children bounce back at a fast rate."

"And will there be a lot of follow-up visits?"

Cate's brow furrowed. What was Luc fishing for? Was he really this interested? Or was something on his mind?

"If things go as planned, we'll do one about a month after and then we won't need to see her for another year."

"So, if she was living forty minutes outside Denver in a quiet place where she could recuperate—no germs being shared at day care—you don't think that would be a problem? She wouldn't be too far from medical care?" Luc's questions came out in a rush, and Cate's jaw lunged for her toes.

What was Luc doing? What was he thinking? *Was* he attempting to take Ruby from her?

Had she said those thoughts out loud earlier? Or had Luc plucked them from her mind? Eerie. It was as if she'd allowed the truth to surface for one moment, and Luc had immediately set about making her nightmares come true. Her throat closed off, and she couldn't speak over the lump of outraged tears she refused to release.

"We'll know more after the procedure, but I don't think Dr. Thom would have any issues with that. Our patients come from all over the place. Not everyone lives in town."

Cate resisted a hiss at her answer. At Luc's audacity.

And one look at Ruby made it all a thousand times worse. Her headphones were looped around her neck, not on her ears. By the way her face perked with interest, she'd heard everything Luc had just asked. Ruby might not know exactly what Luc was saying, but she knew it involved her.

Who did Luc think he was, throwing out preposterous ideas in front of Ruby like he was…like he was her father and had a say in her life? Ruby couldn't just be uprooted. She had a schedule. Day care. Friends. Luc might not see those things—or Cate—as important, but she did.

Ruby bounced with excitement. "What is it, Mommy? Are we going somewhere?"

Red flames had to be shooting out of the top of Cate's head. Her face radiated with heat, now likely the shade of a scarlet crayon.

Cate sought with everything in her to manage a calm tone. "We'll have to discuss it, sweets." Gaze bouncing from Ruby, she raised a menacing eyebrow at Luc. "As a family." Voice wobbling with barely suppressed anger, she focused on breathing as Diane wrapped up the visit and left.

At Cate's direction, Ruby grabbed her

small backpack of supplies from the corner of the room.

Gripping Luc's arm, Cate lowered her voice. "What are you thinking? That I won't care if Ruby comes to live with you? She has a life, Lucas. I realize I kept her from you, but trying to take her from me isn't the answer."

Stunned silence came from Luc. His mouth hung open, much like Cate's had only minutes before.

"I got the big hostable door open!" Ruby stood with her back propping open the wide door, pride evident.

They exclaimed what a good job she did, then followed Ruby down the beige hallway, friction wedged between them like a third wheel.

Luc pulled her behind Ruby's pace. Out of earshot. "I'm not…" His head shook as if he was clearing away cobwebs. "You think I'm trying to take her from you?"

What else was she supposed to think?

"I don't want to separate the two of you. Even I know that's out of the question, Cate. What kind of ogre do you think I am?"

Thankfully, he didn't wait for her to answer.

"I've just been thinking that if you and Ruby would be willing to live at the ranch, even for just a few weeks or a month, it would allow me time to get to know her. We have guests six days out of the week during the summer. If you don't, it will be really hard for me to get away and spend time with her. I'll make it work, somehow, but…it was just a thought." His voice lowered. Hardened. "And I am not such an idiot or jerk that I think she'd be coming alone. I do realize that she's young and the two of you are a package. I wouldn't do that to her."

Now it was her turn to fumble for words. Luc caught up with Ruby, leaving Cate a few steps behind. Good. She needed the space to deal with…everything. Luc's absurd suggestion. Her desire to scream *no* at his back. Or maybe throw something at those annoyingly broad shoulders filling out a cornflower blue short-sleeved button-down.

He was wrong, right? She didn't have to truly consider what he was asking for, did she?

Not one part of her wanted to uproot their lives to live at the ranch, even for a short amount of time. But since Luc was acting so...so *calm* about all of it—even logical, if she wanted to give him credit for that, which she didn't—Cate probably should try to be, too.

Or at least pretend to be. Right before she told him absolutely not.

Chapter Four

The smell of hospital antiseptic assaulted Luc's nostrils. He hated the scent of anything bleached or overly sterilized. Growing up on a ranch with dirt under his fingernails and dust on his boots, he firmly believed that being covered in or even ingesting a little of God's good earth wouldn't harm a person.

Of course, the fact that he was in the hospital waiting for his daughter to get out of surgery could probably explain his current aversion.

Cate had been as quiet as a teapot just

under boiling all morning. He kept wondering when she'd blow. Tears. An outburst. Any show of emotion. But so far, not one crack in her shell.

When they'd prepped Ruby for surgery, they'd given her something to make her groggy and almost fall asleep before doing the anesthesia. He and Cate had been allowed to walk her back to the catheterization area, and then the medical staff had taken Ruby from there.

Luc had thought Cate would crumble in that moment. And it had looked like she was about to. Her shoulders had slumped, eyes glazing over with pain and moisture. He'd been ready to catch her. To comfort her. No matter what had happened between them, he wouldn't hold their history against her at such an agonizing time.

But then Cate had stitched herself together like a desperate woman out on the trail. Bleeding and alone with no other choice.

Even though he'd been standing right next to her.

It had been like watching a storm roll over the mountains, dark and menacing, only to see it morph into white, harmless clouds that floated by without wreaking havoc.

Cate had stridden by him, shoulders back, stubborn chin thrust out. Down the hallway and into the waiting room she'd gone. She'd dropped into a chair and hadn't moved yet. Not even to use the restroom.

Now she sat next to him with her eyes closed in the unforgiving chairs that boasted cushions but didn't offer comfort. He knew she wasn't sleeping. He'd guess she was coping about as well as one of the consistently used children's books Emma had for Kids' Club. Battered. Worn. With the pages barely holding together under the still-intact cover.

The ticking of the plain-Jane white clock with black hands in the corner marked the excruciatingly slow passage of time.

"You okay?" He finally ruptured the silence, questioning Cate.

"No, I'm not okay." Her voice snapped, but then her chestnut eyes flashed open, filled with regret. "I'm sorry." She toyed with the silver ring sporting a cross on her right hand, concentrating on it instead of him. "I'm just worried."

It was the first chink in her armor that he'd witnessed. Capable Cate made raising Ruby on her own look easy. Like even single parenthood couldn't deflate the wind in her cape.

"I am, too." The dull ache in his gut had been there for days, reminding him of Ruby's impending procedure.

Cate's brow pinched. "Then why do you seem so calm?"

Funny. Didn't she realize how composed she looked and acted? Something about knowing she wasn't—that she'd confided even that small secret to him—twisted his insides.

"I'm not, really. But I'm choosing to believe she's going to be okay. That's what I've been praying nonstop for." He wasn't going to entertain any other options.

Her lips barely managed a curve. "Me, too."

Had Cate slept at all last night? Drifting off had taken him much longer than normal. And then he'd been up before the sun to get here on time. Hints of tired were visible despite Cate's perfectly applied makeup—not too much, not too little. Her clothes—black jeans, flats and a peach sleeveless shirt partially covered by a button-up gray sweater—shouted that she had it all together. Her protective covering was in place, but her weariness was palpable. At least to him.

"I don't know what I'd do without her." Cate's hand pressed against her mouth. Luc wasn't sure if it was to stifle a sob or because she'd realized what she'd said—and that Luc had, because of her, lived without Ruby for the past three-plus years.

He bit down on the *I know what you mean*

that begged for escape. Today was not the day for fighting. Things might not be fixed between them, but the seriousness of Ruby's procedure had caused him to mentally call a time-out from his anger.

He was by no means over what Cate had done in keeping Ruby from him, but he was praying that God would help him to be one day. That kind of forgiveness would have to come from above.

But he did have an idea of what might help heal his wounds. And since they were just sitting here, listening to the unbearably slow seconds tick by...

"Cate, I really think you should consider—"

"You're not going to start bugging me about us moving to the ranch again, are you?"

So much for his stealth move in bringing it up. "It just makes sense. We have guests all week right now and it will be tough for me to see Ruby as much as I want to. It will be easier for me to swing it during the off-season." Of course, he would make it work to see Ruby no matter what, but if Cate would just consider the option, it would be a huge help. "You could contact her day care. See if they could give you a credit for the month. It would save money. My sisters are there— Mackenzie is—" determined, stubborn "— all about adventure and Emma's a rock star with kids. You'd have family. Support. It wouldn't be forever. Just enough time for me to get to know Ruby a little bit better."

A groan came from Cate.

"Is that a yes?"

This time a huff escaped, sounding sky-high on the annoyed meter. Guess she hadn't appreciated his attempt at humor.

"It's a no. The same no I've been telling you since we met with the nurse." Her arms criss-crossed her chest, another shield engaged and ready for battle. "And stop sending me pictures. They're not going to change my mind."

He curbed a grin, deciding his amusement

definitely wouldn't be appreciated. Cate had texted him yesterday morning after he'd bugged her plenty about the option of them temporarily moving to the ranch—*please stop talking to me about the ranch.*

So he'd switched to pictures. He hadn't *said* anything, so he hadn't broken any rules. Until today.

Luc had hoped the visuals might stir something in her. He'd sent her a shot of the cabin they could live in. His—but he'd happily give it up for them. It had two bedrooms, a cozy living room with a fireplace, stackable laundry and a tiny kitchen consisting of a row of kitchen cabinets and small appliances. But since the ranch provided all meals, Cate wouldn't need much space for cooking. Not that she had anything much bigger now. And the cabin was certainly better than the apartment she and Ruby currently lived in. At least in his mind.

He'd also sent her pictures of the horses— that one may not have helped—and of the wide open spaces he considered one of the most beautiful places on planet Earth. He didn't think he'd gotten very far since Cate had simply stopped responding to the photos. Stubborn woman.

"If Ruby bugging me hasn't worked, nothing will. And trust me, she's talked about it nonstop since you dropped the idea on us. Thank you very much for that." She shifted in his direction, jutting a finger at his chest. "Parenting 101—don't say anything in front of a child until it's already been decided. You can't just go around spouting ideas like that. She'll never understand why we're not doing it, and I'll be the bad guy. We have a life, Lucas. We can't just uproot it."

Lucas. Why his full name coming from her lips caused a spark in his chest, he didn't want to know.

"But your work is freelance. You can live anywhere."

Cate's eyelids shuttered as if weighted down. "Let's not do this today, okay?"

Regret flared to life. She was right. Not the time.

Luc stretched his jean-clad legs out in front of him but couldn't get comfortable. He'd worn his Ariat boots today. A green button-down shirt. Something about the hospital—or *hostable*, as Ruby would say—made him feel like a kid playing grown-up, and he'd at least attempted to look the part.

"Can I get you anything? Something to eat? Drink?" Why did he feel the need to keep talking? It wasn't like him. If Luc had to guess, he'd imagine he was more apprehensive about Ruby's procedure than he wanted to admit. Taking care of Cate—scratch that—getting something for Cate would occupy his mind and harness his energy. He'd much rather be doing than sitting.

"No. Thanks. I can't imagine eating anything right now." Her hair was in a low bun today, a pair of simple silver earrings in her ears.

She slid a thumbnail between her lips. Luc had only seen her start to bite her nails once since she'd waltzed back into his life almost two weeks ago. That time she'd quit as soon as she'd noticed what she was doing. Her nails looked nice—painted a soft pink. She must make an effort not to engage the old habit.

He snagged her hand to stop her from wrecking what she'd accomplished, but once it was in his grasp, he wasn't sure what to do. Let go? Hold on? He'd only been wanting to help her. Instead, his mind stuttered like an old, rusty engine at her touch. It had been a long, long time since he'd felt Cate's skin against his. Her hand was incredibly soft compared to his, and he caught the faint scent of a lotion or perfume he remembered her using. Something fresh. Reminded him of a field of wildflowers.

She snatched her fingers away from him,

and after a glare in his direction, she shifted so that she sat on both of her hands.

All right, then. Guess that answered that question.

"Catherine Malory?" a voice called from the entrance to the waiting room, and both he and Cate bolted from their seats. They reached the surgeon, and at the last second, the hand Cate had just torn away from his found him again. Surprise rippled through him.

He didn't say anything. Just squeezed and held on, wanting to lend Cate support. She probably didn't even realize her actions.

"Is she okay?" Cate asked before the surgeon had time to speak, her question so rushed it reminded Luc of Ruby.

Dr. Thom's reassuring nod had Luc releasing a pent-up breath. "She did great. Everything went well. You can head back to see her in a couple of minutes."

Cate dropped his hand like a rock. It

crashed to his side as she palmed her face, relief and tears mingling.

The quick dismissal of his services—of any connection—left Luc scrambling to catch up. Would this be his new role? Needed one moment, held at a ten-mile distance the next? With the second being the much more common scenario.

Would Cate ever truly let him into Ruby's life? And hers? Because he knew the two were intertwined. He wouldn't have a place with Ruby unless Cate admitted him entrance. Right now he was nothing more than a useless horse sent out to pasture. A backup plan. And if his instincts were right, an unwanted one, at that.

Cate scanned the premade salads in the hospital cafeteria cooler, the choices as jumbled as algebra. Ruby had been out of surgery for about two hours and doing well. She'd been in pain when she'd first woken up. The entry site in her leg plus the general anesthesia had left her disgruntled, but after the nurse had adjusted her medicine, she'd settled down. Cate had been thankful to see her drift back to sleep. Once she had, Cate had left Luc standing guard.

She'd needed a moment. Time to calm her jittery body with deep breaths and prayers of thankfulness for a successful procedure. So far it still hadn't listened.

Her stomach clamored for something to edge out her nervous hunger. It wanted an extra-large piece of chocolate cake, but she planned to ignore that emotional request.

Everything in Cate's oversize brown leather bag was Ruby-oriented. She'd forgotten to bring anything she might want to eat. Forgotten to take care of herself. Forgivable on a day like today.

She grabbed a chicken kale salad and turned to go, then thought better of it and perused the sandwiches. Luc would likely be hungry, too. Did he still eat like he had at nineteen? Back then he'd been able to clean off three plates in one sitting without adding an inch to his lean frame.

She'd certainly fallen fast and hard for Luc. They'd met at a party at a friend's house. After talking for a few hours that night, he'd asked for her number.

They'd had coffee. And then dinner. He'd been so good about getting to know her that by the time she'd figured out she was in love with him, she'd been miles downstream with no chance of swimming back. Not that she'd wanted to. Sure, they'd had their moments of immaturity. Luc had been quick-tempered back then. A verbal fighter. Always wanting to be right. And she'd only been too willing to get in the ring with him. But despite some childish arguments, Luc had made her feel loved in a way no one ever really had before. Adored even. Like she was the best thing that had ever happened to him.

She missed that. Missed what they'd once been.

Cate selected a club sandwich, knowing

Luc wasn't picky enough to complain, and headed to the checkout. She paid, cringing at the exorbitant prices, and returned to Ruby's room. She didn't want her girl to wake up and not have her there. Though now that they had Luc—now that Ruby had her father—Cate wasn't the only one carrying the load of responsibility on her shoulders. Ruby had someone else to depend on.

At the door to Ruby's room, Cate paused. Luc was in a chair close to the bed, his elbows propped against the mattress. Shoulders hunched. Head in his hands. It looked like he was praying. Ruby slept peacefully, eyelashes grazing her soft cheeks.

The dam Cate had built strong and tight in order to survive today burst free, one weak little chink at a time. It was obvious that Luc loved Ruby. He didn't hold back with her. Had pursued her diligently since finding out the test results. They talked every night for at least a few minutes, usually as Cate was putting Ruby to bed. So of course she heard them on her phone. They were already crazy about each other.

And Cate had been the one who'd kept them apart. Yes, she'd thought she had the right to do what she did. Even believed she was doing the best thing for Ruby. But that didn't make the reality of her choices any easier to swallow.

Cate had been scared of losing her daughter or fighting over Ruby like her own parents had over her. But she had to move past that now. Somehow. It wasn't right that her fears had kept the two of them apart.

Even if Luc had started seeing someone else at the end of their relationship, she should have let him be a part of Ruby's life. And Cate didn't even know if that was true. He'd denied any wrongdoing.

Luc deserved time with Ruby. Deserved to know his daughter like Cate did.

Tears of acknowledgment swept down her cheeks. She was going to have to give in to Luc's request about their living at the ranch temporarily.

Cate's head shook, sending more moisture cascading. Why did God always ask her for the toughest things? The ones she couldn't do. At least not without His strength.

Truly, Cate didn't know if it was God or guilt nudging her, but either way, they were both right. She'd already taken enough from Luc. She didn't need to cause more harm.

Retrieving a tissue from her purse, she swiped away the mascara that had surely loosened with her emotions, then stuffed the tissue back inside.

Her footsteps into the room caused Luc to straighten and turn. He rubbed a hand through his hair, eyes blinking as though they'd been closed.

"Brought you something to eat." She tossed him the packaged sandwich, and he caught it.

"Thanks." Surprise was quickly replaced by gratitude.

Cate stopped directly in front of him, and he studied her, faint concern etching his brow. His jean-clad legs and boots were tucked under the chair. The green button-down shirt he wore made the fern in his hazel eyes pop.

"Have you been crying?"

Her eyes rolled at being so easily caught. Frustrating. They always gave her away. She dug up a smile, albeit a wobbly one. "I'm fine. Just releasing some pent-up stress from today."

His mouth stayed in a firm line. He nodded toward Ruby. "She's been asleep the whole time."

"Good." Cate forced herself to speak. "Okay."

Confusion evident, Luc's head cocked to one side. "Okay, what?"

She could do this. She could put on her big-girl britches and do the right thing. "We'll live at the ranch for a few weeks."

His jaw slacked. Suddenly, he was out of

the chair, standing way too close for comfort, hands squeezing her upper arms. "Are you serious?" She wanted to tell him to turn his booming voice down a notch but simply nodded instead.

He whooped and scooped her up in a hug. A very unacceptable, he-did-not-have-permission hug. Cate would try to break free, but she wasn't a match for his strength. Plus, when was the last time she'd been held like this? Probably with the man currently rendering her nerves and muscles the consistency of pudding.

He let her down slowly, as if realizing the predicament he'd put them in. Once her feet were firmly back on the ground, his arms dropped to his sides, but neither of them moved from their close proximity.

"Thank you."

He smelled like the outdoors somehow, even within the walls of the hospital. His face was freshly shaved, and for one wild moment she considered sliding her fingers along his smooth jaw. She'd always liked a clean shave on him.

Enough! Cate mentally slapped away her impetuous hand.

Instead of answering him with *you're welcome*, she went with, "I'm sorry."

He nodded once. "I can tell."

Luc might not be forgiving her, but he recognized her remorse. That had to be a good sign.

"Mom? Dad?" Ruby's groggy voice interrupted them. "I want a huggle, too."

Cate's skin heated, but Luc just chuckled and stepped back from her, flashing a magnetizing grin before facing their daughter. He should really be more careful with that thing. Only use it for special occasions. Ruby's first dance. Inheriting a million dollars.

"Guess what, Rube-i-cube?" Elation oozed from him, the nickname he'd coined for Ruby earning a lilting of their daughter's lips. "Your mom has some news to tell you."

Chapter Five

Three days later Cate reached into the open trunk of her car for a box to carry into the cabin, using the few moments alone to shake off the bad attitude that had trailed her along the dusty drive to the ranch.

She might be doing the right thing, but that didn't make it easy.

Scary was a better word.

"We're a lot to handle, aren't we?" Luc's younger sister, Emma, approached Cate, bursting her momentary bubble of solitude.

Dressed in cutoff jean shorts, flip-flops and a Wilder Ranch tank with her hair in a ponytail, everything about Emma reminded Cate of a beauty-product commercial. One with a girl washing her face and then glancing into the mirror, all fresh-skinned and bright-eyed.

In the short time since they'd become acquainted, Cate had come to the swift decision that she liked Emma. Luc's little sister had a cashmere-like demeanor. A sweetness so noticeable it practically radiated from her tiny pores. Unlike his twin sister, Mackenzie, whom Cate had met when they'd arrived today.

Mackenzie had studied Cate like a college art project deserving a failing grade. And it didn't help that the woman was a superhero. Inches taller than Cate, all tanned muscles and an imposing figure in jeans, boots and a fitted gray T-shirt that pronounced to the world that she couldn't care less about fashion but managed to look like an amazon woman anyway. Cate wouldn't be surprised if she'd zip-lined down from the mountains just to help her move in.

Cate wasn't jealous. After all, Mackenzie was Luc's twin sister. But she could classify herself as a bit intimidated.

"I don't know if I'd say that." She finally answered Emma, settling on something diplomatic.

"You don't have to," Emma said, flashing equally commercial-worthy white teeth. "I'll say it for you." She nodded toward the house a short ways down the hill that Mackenzie had just entered. "She'll come around. Mackenzie and Lucas have this weird twin intuition. It'll drive a person nuts, but they'd do anything for each other. She's just protective of him."

Cate hefted the box of Ruby's favorite snack foods out of the trunk. "And I'm to blame because I didn't tell Luc about Ruby." Why had she just said that? This whole situation was uncomfortable enough without her bringing up awkward truths.

Snagging the extra-large duffel bag filled with Cate's clothes, Emma swung it over her shoulder before filling her arms with another bag. "I remember what my brother was like back then. Short on patience. Not always easy to get along with. I imagine for you to go through all of the trouble of raising Ruby yourself, you probably had a pretty good reason."

Cate's eyes pricked with liquid emotion. Emma had thrown her a lifeline, and she wasn't going to be so stubborn as to not take hold. "Thank you."

Luc had told her Emma had just turned twenty-three. Twenty months younger than Luc and Mackenzie and mature well beyond her years.

The two of them headed for the cabin. "So where's Luc staying while we're here?" He hadn't told Cate any details. "Another cabin? Or with you or Mackenzie?"

"With us." She jutted her head toward the house Mackenzie had entered. "He'd probably choose another cabin over us. Jerk. But they're all full."

"Wow." Cate wrestled open the screen door, holding it for Emma as she went through and then following herself. "I'm sorry for forcing him on you two. Taking up your space."

Emma's easy laugh turned into a snort. "Puh-lease! You brought me a niece. No apologies allowed."

God, did You know I'd need this girl? This welcome? Cate sent up a prayer of thanks as her mouth curved to match Emma's. Ruby's new aunt was good for the soul.

They both put their items down, Cate on the counter to be sorted into cupboards if she could find space, and Emma leaving the clothes with a pile of bags, suitcases, boxes and other items Cate and Ruby had deemed necessary for the next few weeks. They planned to head back to Denver the first Sunday in September since Cate had a meeting that Tuesday with the firm she did freelance for. That way they'd have Monday—Labor Day—at home before jumping back into day care and their normal schedule. She and Ruby would be here just shy of a month.

"The guest-ranch business must be doing really well." And Luc must really want them here to give up his place for them. Why did he have to be so kind? Cate should be paying penance for her sins. But no matter how many times she reminded herself that wasn't how God operated, her brain had the hardest time comprehending the concept of grace.

"It is." Emma stretched one arm over her head, then the other. "Luc does a great job keeping us booked up and running well. Mackenzie, too. We've even earned the Top Twenty Guest Ranch Award twice."

Emma made no mention of her own involvement, but Cate knew from their brief encounter at the ranch that she was phenomenal with kids. Ruby had talked quite a bit about her after their visit. She'd referred to her as "that really nice lady that showed me the horsies." Emma had made a big impression on Ruby in a short amount of time.

"I *think* you forgot someone." Cate pointed an accusing finger as she took a cue from Emma and rolled her neck, muscles complaining about the past few days of hurried packing while taking care of Ruby. "Luc says you really have a gift with kids, and I've seen it firsthand with Ruby. She already adores you. You're very sweet with her."

Emma's eyes lit up, a faint rose color dusting her cheeks at the compliment. "How could anyone not instantly fall for Ruby?"

Cate had been afraid to let Luc—and his family—into Ruby's life for years...but she was starting to thaw. To see the advantages of more people loving her little girl.

"Somebody wants a new place to rest." Luc came out of Ruby's room with her in his arms, an unnecessary ride that their daughter had likely instigated. They'd been given very few limitations for Ruby—basically letting the entry site heal—but they planned to have her take it easy for at least a week. Okay, Cate planned to. Just to make sure she was healed and whole.

Dr. Thom had said the surgery went wonderfully, but Cate might need some time to believe it.

"Says she was bored in there. So the couch it is." Luc deposited Ruby on the sofa, rearranging pillows to make her comfortable. "I'll grab your orange thingy."

Her giggle filled the room. "Dad, it's an Apple. A mini iPad."

"Are you sure it's not a banana?"

Another titter from Ruby.

Emma shook her head, one corner of her mouth inching up. "Oy with the dad jokes."

"What's that supposed to mean?" Luc questioned. "What's a dad joke?"

"Anything lame and not that funny. So basically…you."

At Emma's retort, amusement bubbled in

Cate from a place long forgotten. It felt good to laugh.

Luc's eyes narrowed. "I don't like the two of you in cahoots." His scowl wobbled, fighting a curve.

Mackenzie reentered the cabin carrying the last thing from Cate's car—a laundry basket of folded clothes. A cold rush of air accompanied her instead of the August heat. She wasn't *exactly* an ice queen. But her protectiveness of Luc could be spotted from miles away.

Cate understood it. She'd probably be the same way in Mackenzie's boots.

Mackenzie set the basket down and knelt in front of Ruby by the couch, handing her a small wooden box that had been perched on top of the clothes. "This was mine when I was a little girl." She removed the flat wooden doll and showed Ruby how the little pieces of doll clothes could be moved and changed to create different looks. "Now it's yours."

"Really?" Ruby lit up like a Christmas tree the day after Thanksgiving.

"Yep." A rarely bestowed smile framed Mackenzie's face. It was like spotting an endangered animal. A beautiful creature that only surfaced at night. Or in search of prey.

In true Ruby fashion, she went in for a hug. At first hesitant, Mackenzie's arms quickly tightened.

Cate's heart turned to crème brûlée, the crisp shell giving way to the soft custard beneath. If there was a way to win her respect, it was by seeing Ruby for the sweet, wonderful girl she was. Tough-as-nails Mackenzie had found the key. And the fact that she wasn't letting her obvious concern over Cate affect her relationship with Ruby meant Cate's regard for her just shot up another ten notches.

"Anything else you need me to get from the car?" Luc entered Cate's personal space as he asked, sending off those pesky alarms again. He wore a simple blue Wilder Ranch

T-shirt boasting their *get out in the wild* tagline, jeans and boots. And he managed to make it look photo-shoot worthy. How was that possible? And why did she stay attracted to him like a magnet when she'd told herself numerous times to stop already?

Space. Cate needed a few miles of separation between them right about now. Was it too late to hop back into her car and escape?

"I don't think so. Pretty sure Mackenzie got the last of it." She busied herself with a few of Ruby's snacks, tucking them into surprisingly empty cupboards. Luc must depend on the communal meals for most of his nourishment.

He stayed still, watching her. Luc had a habit of noticing her. She wasn't sure what to make of it. It was hard to be next to him and not wonder about them. The "them" that had existed before Ruby. Before that last awful fight. But then, she'd promised herself she wouldn't go anywhere near that kind of thought pattern. Ruby came first, and Cate wasn't about to let herself fall in and out of a relationship with Ruby's father. She knew too well from her parents' example how that ended. Yet another lesson they'd graciously demonstrated.

"Dinner is at six at the lodge." Mackenzie paused by the door before leaving. "I left my cell number for you, but coverage can be spotty. Emma and I are here if you need anything." Serious blue-gray eyes met Cate's—the kind that saw all and dissected before coming to a conclusion—their message clear. Mackenzie might not be ready to forgive Cate for what she'd done to Luc, but Ruby wouldn't suffer because of it. Cate got the impression she could count on Mackenzie for just about anything regarding Ruby and the woman would come through, superhero muscles not even sporting a scratch.

Comforting thought. If Emma was made of love and wispy cotton candy, Mackenzie was built of steely strength. Both were good to have in her corner.

"Thank you." Funny how much they'd just communicated without speaking.

"I'm going, too," Emma piped up. "The afternoon Kids' Club starts in a few minutes." She gave Cate a quick hug, like it was a normal, everyday occurrence and didn't make her breath catch in her throat like it did in Cate's. The simple gesture warmed Cate in a place that had frozen over years before. Around the time when Luc had walked out of her life. Her heart had shattered when she'd told him to leave and never contact her again—and he'd listened. Now it was like a puzzle on the thrift-store shelf with torn edges and missing pieces.

"Thank you for your help," she called after the two women. Her voice quickly faded, leaving only the sounds of the show Ruby watched.

Luc stood still as a statue, glancing between her and Ruby.

"Don't you need to go?"

"Yes. But I can find someone else to cover

the shooting range. One of the wranglers can handle it."

And then what? Luc would stay here with her and Ruby? No, thank you.

Cate jutted her chin in Ruby's direction. "She's doing really great, Luc. I'll just let her watch something while I unpack and get my computer set up. You go do your thing and we'll see you for dinner."

That sounded like a date.

"At the lodge," she added. With lots and lots of other people.

His breath rushed out. "Okay. Call me if you need anything. I'll have my cell turned way up, but since they don't always work, I can check in on you girls after—"

"We're fine." Cate infused some Mackenzie-like steel into her voice. "That's only a few hours away. You don't need to check on us this afternoon." She placed her hands on his shoulders, turning him toward the door like a little kid's spin top. Heat met her fingertips through his T-shirt, and she cast her eyes toward the ceiling to avoid concentrating on his shortly cropped hair that begged for her attention. Or touch. "Time to go away now." She shoved lightly, knowing her strength might not propel him physically, but he should get the picture.

A quiet chuckle shook his back, and Luc raised his hands in defeat. After calling out a goodbye to Ruby, he was gone.

Cate indulged in a supersize inhalation that felt like the first in days, releasing it slowly.

Why did his presence make her feel so... jittery? The illusion of safety and yet hopped up on caffeine at the same time. But Luc was nowhere near safe. In the beginning he might have been, but then she'd fallen too hard and loved him too much. That got a person in trouble.

Cate couldn't make decisions based on emotion. Ruby needed her to be logical and steer clear of any thoughts revolving around a relationship with Luc.

"Mom, can I have some juice?"

"Sure." She got out the apple juice and added some to Ruby's cup, topping it with the lid and straw.

After her parents' divorce, there'd been a short time—about a year later—when they'd attempted a reconciliation. Not that they'd told her. But Cate had been eleven and not as oblivious as they imagined. She'd sat on the stairs, hearing their laughter. The clinking of wineglasses. Hope had ignited as she'd slunk back up to bed at her mom's house. Could they really be a family again? It was every kid's dream. But Cate should have known better, even at that age. A few short weeks later it was heated voices that rose and fell. New arguments. And even more tension and viciousness than when the divorce first happened. It had almost been harder for Cate the second time around. Taking any dream of them reuniting that she'd secretly harbored and running it through the paper shredder of life.

Her parents had taught her exactly what happened when feelings led the way. Logic was, by far, the better choice. When Cate had been nineteen and in love with Luc, she'd had all of the first and none of the second. And just look how that had turned out.

She passed the juice to Ruby, running a hand over her forehead and smoothing her hair back. "I'm not going to do that to you, sweets."

Ruby looked up. "What, Mommy?"

"Nothing." Cate managed a shaky smile.

Ruby might not be able to keep her emotional distance from Luc—and she shouldn't—but Cate could. She could protect herself. They might be living at the ranch for Ruby and Luc's sake, but that was the only concession Cate planned to make.

Luc pushed away from his desk. Paperwork. Bills. Bookkeeping. These were his least favorite parts of the job, but they were important. Which was why he forced himself to do them when he'd rather be out leading a trail ride or doing any of the other outdoor activities.

The week since Ruby and Cate had arrived had flown by, and Luc had gotten to spend time with Ruby each day. He popped over to their cabin as much as he could between responsibilities. Ate meals with them every day.

Since he had a few minutes and the numbers in front of him had started swimming, he'd head up to see her now. He wanted to take advantage of Ruby's presence at the ranch. Couldn't help feeling like the time would be over with the snap of his fingers.

His phone beeped with a text as he walked the gravel path that snaked through thirsty grass. His mom.

Praying for you today, hon. Be who God is asking you to be in this situation. He'll give you peace and wisdom.

Luc had told his parents about Ruby after the test came back positive. They'd been shocked, of course. He understood the sentiment well. In the days since, they'd been trying to wrap their minds around the situation and had also been praying for him, Ruby and Cate. It meant a lot to him that they weren't completely freaking out. Not that he knew that for sure. His mom was an interesting mix of calm and protective mama bear. She'd likely be full of more and more questions as time progressed. Ones Luc didn't have answers to. He was flying by the seat of his pants. Or maybe the better way to say it would be, following God blindly.

He knocked quietly on the cabin door in case Ruby was sleeping. Though she hadn't been napping much at all. Cate said before surgery, she got tired a lot faster. But her energy levels had gone up since the procedure. That had to be a good sign.

No one answered the door. Luc eased it

open an inch and called out in a loud whisper. "Cate." Still nothing. He edged it farther and heard Cate's voice.

Sounded like she might be on the phone in the bedroom. Luc stepped inside and caught part of her discussion about colors and a vector file—not that he had a clue what that last thing was. Must be work related.

He'd just say hi to Ruby and then be out of here.

She was on the far side of the living room, playing with her colorful ponies under the back window.

"Ruby." He said her name quietly, hoping he wouldn't scare her.

In response, Prim gave a snarly meow from the kitchen sink, arching her back. The cat had taken to napping—or perhaps just hiding—in the sink. Almost as if she was waiting for Luc to enter the cabin so she could scare the living daylights out of him.

But that couldn't be, could it?

Either way, he definitely had not won over the feline's affections.

Ruby's head swung in his direction, eyes widening with excitement. She crossed the room in a flat-out run to give him a hug, and he swung her into his arms, not sure he'd ever get used to a greeting like that. By far the best part of his day.

"How's my girl?"

"I want to go play with the horsies, but Mommy said I have to stay here while she does her meeting." Her mouth formed a pout. A cute one. Ruby wore jean shorts and a purple T-shirt, her bare toes sporting bright pink nail polish. "I don't want to stay in the cabin anymore."

At first, Cate had wanted Ruby to lie low until the incision site healed. But it definitely had. And despite Cate's lingering worries, Ruby was over being cooped up.

Luc didn't blame her. He'd always been far more comfortable outside than in.

He also didn't blame Cate. She had work

to do, and he'd told her they'd be a help not a hindrance. At this point Ruby could be back in day care and Cate would have time to accomplish her projects without interruption. Luc didn't want Cate frustrated and scrambling out of here before their planned departure date. He'd ask Emma if there was room for Ruby in Kids' Club. And Luc could keep her with him for a bit of time each day. That way Cate would have the hours she needed for work and not want to tear out of here before the month was up.

"I think I have a cure for that. Why don't you come with me for a little bit?"

Ruby's head bobbed.

"Or you can go with your aunt Emma and the other kids. I'm sure she'd love to have you."

The nodding increased. "I want to do that."

"Which one?"

"Aunt Emma."

Luc would be more offended that she'd

chosen Emma if his sister wasn't so amazing with kids. He'd pick her, too.

"Get your shoes on and we'll go."

He plunked her down, and Ruby disappeared into her room. Luc could still hear Cate on the phone, and he didn't want to interrupt by text or in person, so he scavenged in the junk drawer for a piece of paper and a pen. He wrote a note, then tried to figure out where to put it so she'd see it.

The cabin was immaculate. A vase of wildflowers decorated the kitchen countertop, a marshmallow-scented candle burning next to it. And on the fireplace mantel, she'd displayed a number of small, clear glasses he recognized from the cupboard, filling them with branches and other greenery. Things he never would have put together but that now looked like they should go in an art show.

Cate had been here for one week and she'd already managed to make the cabin into more of a home than he ever had. Luc had kept things tidy, but she made him look like a slob. The counters were gleaming. Even the small toaster had been stored.

He opened a cupboard and spied some crackers. He set the box on the edge of the counter closest to the bedroom and propped the note against it. That would have to do. Surely Cate would see something out of place right when she walked out.

Ruby was back at his side in no time at all wearing pink sandals. Luc wasn't sure that worked for what Emma had on the schedule for today, but it would have to do.

He'd need to get Ruby some boots if she planned to grow up on a ranch. Except… she wasn't going to, was she? Luc was living in a fairy tale his daughter would watch in one of her movies if he thought that was a possibility.

Cate had agreed to stay at the ranch for a few weeks on a temporary basis. Probably out of guilt. The rest of Ruby's life would be torn between two places.

He hated the thought of that.

"I'm ready." Ruby tugged on his hand.

He was nowhere near ready to let go of her. Never would be. Course, Ruby was talking now, and Luc was jumping into the future. She'd just gotten here—the ranch and his life. He needed to take things one day at a time. "Then let's go."

They walked down the path, dust rising under their shoes and joined hands. Ruby chatted at the speed of light while Luc contemplated how to repair something that wasn't anywhere near fixable.

Chapter Six

If money didn't matter so much, Cate would send the client across the screen from her packing. He was demanding. Impatient. And sometimes offensive. But she needed the work—always did—so none of the above mattered. Being a single mother didn't allow her the opportunity to be choosy.

"One more thing." Vincent held up a thick pointer finger that came across the screen as menacing. "I know this is the color scheme I said I wanted, but I don't like it." He motioned to the paper in his hand. "I really need you to rework this. And I need it by tomorrow."

Of course he did. Cate indulged in the fantasy of letting go of a long, loud, overdue scream, but she didn't think that would go over well. Vincent was one of her bigger clients. She didn't have a choice. She'd have to turn this job around. Again. And then hunker down to complete the magazine for the Denver Building Association she had due at the end of this week.

Cate clarified a few points, and then the two of them disconnected. She dropped her head to the small table she was using as a desk in the corner of Luc's room—now temporarily hers. Her brain tumbled like a pebble in the drum of a washing machine. If only she could tell Vincent she didn't want to work for him anymore. The man was her least favorite client. Full of last-minute deadlines and changes. But the money was too good to pass up. And she'd definitely charge him for these. She always made him sign off on changes so that she could add additional fees while proving he'd made the requests. And for some reason, he kept hiring her.

Stretching arms over her head, Cate attempted to release the kinks in her neck and unwind her screaming muscles. Stress of any sort made her twist up like a rubber band.

She removed the long silver necklace that she'd worn over a dressy turquoise tank top for the meeting and placed it on the desk. She'd paired the shirt with black skinny ankle pants, wanting to look professional even over the computer screen.

The time in the corner of her computer made her gasp and pop up from her seat. Ruby would be climbing the walls by now. The girl was too social to survive five minutes by herself. Cate was surprised she hadn't popped in once or twice during her Skype call, but then, she had bribed her with a Popsicle if she could occupy herself for the supposed-to-be-half-hour meeting that had morphed into an hour.

The mark of a good parent—bribery. At least that was what Cate told herself. Survival came in all forms.

"Sorry, Rubes." She opened the slightly ajar bedroom door. "I didn't know the meeting would go so long. I owe you big-time, kiddo."

There was no sign of Ruby in the living room or bathroom. Maybe she'd crawled into her bed and decided to take a nap. Ha! Now Cate really was being delusional.

Crossing to the other bedroom, Cate stepped inside the darkened space. No Ruby in the bed. Or under it. Cate's pulse revved as she walked around the bed just to make sure Ruby wasn't hiding on the other side. She checked the closet. Nothing. There was nowhere else Ruby could be in the bedroom, so Cate took off for the living room again.

She scanned the couch and fireplace. Ruby's ponies were set up on a wooden bench under the window. Prim watched Cate from the fireplace hearth.

"Where's Ruby, Prim? Where'd she go?"

This was where a dog might be a better fit than a cat, because Prim's answer was to squint and lick a paw.

Weakness spread through Cate's limbs. The places Ruby could be hiding were diminishing. Just like her attempt at remaining calm.

She checked the bathroom again, this time flipping on the light and yanking back the shower curtain with shaking hands.

Empty.

Cate ran for the front door and ripped it open. The step was vacant, the dirt path barren. Cate had thought maybe Ruby had wanted to sit outside, but there was no sign of her or any of her toys.

She called for Ruby numerous times, volume heightening with each attempt to locate her daughter. No answer.

A fist closed around her throat. Could Ruby be playing a game of hide-and-seek?

Cate tore back into the house, leaving the

front door open in case anyone had heard her calling and offered any help. "Ruby, if you're hiding from me it's not funny anymore. I need you to come out. You're going to get a Popsicle, remember?"

Surely that would do the trick.

But no giggle or small voice answered her. Just an agitated meow from Prim. Cate opened the lower cupboard doors. She couldn't imagine Ruby fitting inside, but it was worth a try. After that she checked the small closet to the side of the front door. The outdoorsy scent of Luc wafted from the coats and sweatshirts that hung in the space. Cate shoved the boots on the floor to the side. No Ruby.

Once again she offered a treat, this time upping the ante to ice cream. But when she didn't receive an answer, her panic shot into the red.

Ruby wasn't here.

The cabin wasn't big enough for her to hide and Cate not to find her. Besides, the girl wasn't that good at hide-and-seek yet. A portion of her body was always visible, sticking out from behind a piece of furniture or shaking with laughter under a blanket.

What should Cate do? Had Ruby wandered out the door? The ranchland was endless. She could be anywhere, surrounded by any number of wild animals. Cate's heart ping-ponged in her chest.

What had Ruby been wearing? Her mind scrounged for the description she'd need to supply to the search-and-rescue crew.

Snagging her phone from her desk, she tried Luc as she walked back into the living room. No answer. Next, she called Mackenzie, impatience mounting with each ring. Maybe she and Emma had seen Ruby or even had her with them.

It *had* to be something simple like that. But while her mind agreed with that logic, her body was too busy mentally assuming the fetal position.

"Hello?" Mackenzie answered just as Cate

spied the note propped against the cracker box on the counter. Luc's writing. She blinked, attempting to focus long enough to read his message.

"Cate? Everything okay?" Funny. Even Mackenzie knew if Cate was calling her, something must be wrong. Only it wasn't.

She scanned the scrap of paper. "No. I mean yes. Everything is okay. False alarm. I—I couldn't find Ruby, but I guess Luc has her."

"Oh, yeah. She's actually with Emma and the other kids at the moment."

Heat engulfed Cate's face, matching the indignation churning inside. "Thanks." She swallowed. Tried to get some moisture back into her mouth. "That helps."

They hung up, and Cate placed her hands against the counter, inhaling long and slow in an attempt to settle her buzzing nervous system.

What had Luc been thinking? Why hadn't he at least popped in and motioned to her or something? Who did he think he was, taking Ruby like he had?

Cate pushed off the counter. She needed to talk to him, and there was no way the conversation could wait until dinner.

"You all set?" Luc questioned Brant, the nineteen-year-old who would lead the afternoon trail ride. The kid had been a godsend when he'd shown up last summer looking for work. He knew more about flowers, birds and anything to do with nature than any of the other leads, and the guests loved him.

"Yeah, dude. Ready to rock."

Dude. Brant was far more snowboarder than cowboy, but he knew these trails in and out. Being a wrangler at the ranch was the perfect fit for him because it meant he had portions of the winter months off and could spend his time on the slopes.

Brant whistled to get the group's attention, then began his short instruction spiel. He tugged on the straps to his backpack while talking, which was loaded with emergency supplies—granola bars and extra water for the guest who forgot theirs. It was important to stay hydrated, as altitude sickness could come on fast and fierce.

"Mr. Wilder, I wanted to ask you about the dance at the end of the week." An older woman with gray hair and squeaky new cowboy boots approached. Those were going to rub some mean blisters into existence by the end of the day.

"Call me Luc… Mrs. Tepa," he finally recalled.

"I don't have any clothes for the dance, not a single dress, and I'm…" She continued talking as Cate stormed down the trail from the cabins, looking like she'd been stung by a bee and was in hot pursuit of blaming… someone.

If he called out *not it*, would she head in another direction and find a different target?

He and Cate had managed to avoid any of the real issues swimming under their bridge this week, but it looked like their raft was about to crash over the falls.

His head shook at the thought.

"So I can't wear casual clothes?" Mrs. Tepa asked.

"Oh, sorry. I wasn't answering you. I—Yes, you can. The dance is casual. Nothing fancy. Boots and jeans make the most sense. That's what everyone wears, ma'am."

The square dance that finished off each week was a highlight for the guests. Luc asked people to fill out a short survey at the end of their stay, and that always ranked as one of the favorite activities. Along with moving the cattle. People loved the thought of doing what had been done in the West for centuries.

"Okay, thank you so much." Mrs. Tepa rejoined the group headed for the corral as Cate zoomed in for a landing. Her narrowed eyes were aimed right at him—no surprise there. Though Luc didn't have a clue what he'd done.

And then she was in front of him, the August sun beating down on them and singeing the back of Luc's neck. He'd forgotten to grab his hat on the way out of the lodge and now regretted it. He could have tipped the brim low to deflect a bit of the self-righteous heat pouring from Cate.

Dressed in fancy work clothes and black sandals, Cate looked like she belonged in a Denver office building instead of kicking up dust on a ranch.

Luc wore a different variation of the same thing every day—boots and jeans. A ranch T-shirt or button-down, depending on the weather. And in the winter, a brown Carhartt coat. What had he ever been thinking, falling crazy in love with this woman? He and Cate had so little in common.

"*What* were you thinking?" Her question mimicked his thoughts. Thankfully, the guests were far enough away that they didn't turn to investigate her snippy, accusatory tone.

"Regarding what?" The two of them had plenty of situations she could be referring to. "Past or present?"

His quip only increased her scowl. "You took my daughter without telling me. I didn't see your note," she spit out, "until after I'd panicked. I thought maybe she was wandering around outside. I didn't know if she was lost or stuck somewhere. And I didn't have a clue where to start looking. It was awful." Her voice wobbled, and her eyelids fluttered like hummingbird wings. Trying to control her emotions? Too bad. Any empathy he might have mustered had deflated with her choice of words.

"*Your* daughter?" If his voice held a bit of malice, sue him. Anger over the decisions Cate had made bubbled as scalding and fierce as the hot spring that sprang up from God's imagination on Wilder land.

Cate's arms crossed in a huff, eyes jutting

to the side as her chin eased forward in defiance. "You know what I mean."

"You're right. I do. You mean Ruby's yours. You might be making a small attempt right now to compromise by staying here, but in a few weeks you're planning to hightail it out of here so fast there'll be a trail of dust a quarter mile wide behind your car. I'm not a fool, Cate. I see what you're doing. You're trying to retain as much control over Ruby as possible while keeping me out."

"I never said that."

"You didn't have to."

This conversation was oddly reminiscent of a fight they would have had when they were younger. Different verse, same chorus. They'd always been feisty with each other— or at least he'd been with her. But their arguing was one of Luc's biggest regrets. If he'd handled those days better and chosen maturity instead of selfishness, maybe he and Cate would still be together. And

Ruby would be *their* daughter. And then he wouldn't have missed the first three-plus years of her life.

No. He wouldn't go down that road again, no matter how much he wanted to be right in this situation. Getting along with the mother of his child was the better choice.

And he certainly hadn't meant to worry Cate.

"I'm sorry."

Her chin jerked back, eyes widening. "What?"

He almost chuckled at her response. He'd thrown her for a loop not continuing to engage in battle with her. Maybe it could be a first step in showing Cate he wasn't that same kid anymore. She would never believe him if his actions didn't back up what he claimed.

"I didn't mean to scare you, taking Ruby. I thought I was helping. I could hear you talking to someone about work, and she was bored. Part of you being here was for us to help, not for you to be working and taking care of Ruby by yourself." He shrugged. "So I asked Ruby if she wanted to stay with me or go with Emma and the kids, and she chose her aunt. Of course."

"Oh." Some of the wind left Cate's sails, though her eyes were still shooting sparks.

"I left you a note."

"I didn't see it right away." Her quiet answer told him she was starting to back down from her high horse, but he needed her to go another few notches before they could have a calm conversation. One without snapping at each other.

"Come with me." Luc hooked a thumb toward the lodge.

"Why?" The woman could sure pack a lot of distrust into one little syllable.

"Do you have to question everything?"

"Yes."

He half laughed, half sighed. Nodded toward the lodge again on his second attempt.

"Do you want a brownie? They're fresh from the oven."

Her lips pressed together, contemplating. Show-off. She didn't have to draw any attention to the spot. He already had it memorized.

"What does that have to do with anything?" Curiosity joined the edge to her voice.

Only Cate could question the motive behind a brownie. "Just come on." He snagged her arm, directing her. If he waited for her to decide, they'd be here all day. His hand felt right at home against her skin, but he ignored the increased rhythm in his chest at being near her. She smelled like flowers and good pieces of the past.

Luc matched his longer stride to Cate's shorter one. He probably had close to half a foot on her in height, but she made up for it in spunk. Case in point: she shook his hand off her arm like she was dealing with an insect instead of a man. His mouth twitched. As long as she kept walking, he wouldn't fight her.

What was it about Cate that both infuriated him and intrigued him at the same time? Just her presence wreaked havoc on him. He wanted to tuck into her and take a good long breath, as if he'd been holding his for the years during their separation and his lungs could finally function again. But he wasn't allowed those kinds of liberties anymore, and he wouldn't take them if he could.

He and Cate had bigger things to focus on than their wayward relationship. Like their daughter. Which was exactly what he wanted to talk to her about.

"Joe made brownies. I could smell them when I was in my office earlier. They're amazing right out of the oven."

Her sideways glance included more narrowing of those caramel eyes. "Are you trying to bribe me into a conversation with the promise of a brownie, Lucas Wilder?"

"Yes, ma'am. That's exactly what I'm doing."

Chapter Seven

The empty kitchen's immaculate stainless-steel countertops and appliances spoke to the neat freak living inside Cate. White fluorescent lights bounced from the surfaces, and the smell of disinfectant from the last meal's cleanup whispered across her senses along with the sweet smell of still-warm chocolate.

Luc went to an open metal shelf lined with rows of filled baking pans and slid one out, placing it on the counter.

"Have a seat." He nodded toward the countertop.

"Won't I get in trouble for that? Isn't that against the rules or something?"

He snagged two small plates, then some silverware from the round metal canisters. "I know the people who run this place. I think you're in the clear." Humor crinkled his cheeks. "Plus, I'm kind of intimidated by Joe. He's been the chef since I was a kid and has reamed me out for being in here more times than I can count. So I'll definitely clean up any mess I make." He glanced at the wall clock. "We have at least thirty minutes before the kitchen staff comes in to start prepping dinner."

Cate pointed to the section of brownies where he'd just cut two large squares from the corner. "That's not going to be a clue?"

His boyish grin grew, causing an ache to echo in her chest. That easy lift of his lips should be illegal. It was too attractive to resist.

After scooping one man-size portion onto the small plastic plate, he handed it to Cate with a fork perched on the side. She touched the top. Felt the warmth.

Setting the plate down, she scooted backward onto the countertop, then picked it back up. This was exactly the kind of thing the old Luc would have made her do. Not quite breaking the rules but not quite following them, either. Good-looking trouble. That was what he was.

She took a bite, the rage that had propelled her in search of Luc melting with the cocoa tantalizing her tongue. This had been a smart move on his part. Not that she was over and done with what had happened.

"Oh, my." She mumbled over the bite of brownie, not in the least bit proper, then swallowed the fudge-like treat. "Are there chocolate chips in these?"

"Yep."

They were still gooey from the oven, and for the moment Cate decided to concentrate on the brownie instead of Luc. She liked one more than she liked the other right now.

Luc slid backward to sit on the counter, too, then picked up his plate. He dug in, and Cate took another forkful, savoring with her eyes closed.

"I take it you still feel the same way about baked goods as you did at nineteen."

His tease held a hint of intimacy. A dance of remembering back to the time when they'd been inseparable and had known all there was to know about each other.

"Maybe." She went with a light answer, unwilling to engage the deeper feelings simmering under the surface. Cate allowed herself another bite, the sugar easing into her system. "Okay, Wilder. You've got me mellowed out. Now what do you want?"

He speared another bite of brownie but left the loaded fork on his plate. "I really didn't mean to upset you about Ruby. I thought you'd see the note. I even pulled a cracker box out of the cupboard to prop it up. The cabin is so neat I thought you'd notice something out of place right away."

She did like having everything clean and orderly. It made her feel safe. In control. Like she could handle the other burning fires if her home life was organized.

Cate could concede that Luc had tried to communicate with her. "I'm surprised I didn't notice. I got done with my meeting and rushed into the living room, but then I couldn't find her anywhere and I just... freaked."

"I'm sorry for that."

"Okay." She could accept his apology. "Thanks."

"You're not used to anyone but you taking care of Ruby."

She mulled over his statement, then decided on acceptance. After all, Luc had chosen not to continue fighting with her when she'd flown at him in full attack mode. "You're right. I'm not."

"That's what I want to talk to you about."

Where was Luc going with this?

"You're holding me back, Cate." His voice

was quiet. Nonconfrontational. But it still stung. "Not necessarily from Ruby, though I would imagine she can sense the turmoil between us. It's funny. You're the one who kept Ruby from me, but it almost feels like…" He set his scraped clean plate down, and it clattered against the metal.

"Like what?" Her voice hitched. She both did and didn't want to know.

"Like you're mad at me."

Oh, boy. A layer of moisture coated her eyes, surprising her. She blinked it away quickly, mind reeling at his statement.

She'd never thought about it before, but he was right.

She *was* mad. About the way it had all ended so horribly. Gutted that he'd left after their fight, no matter what she'd said to him. If he'd been telling her the truth, why hadn't he fought for her? She'd told him to leave, but she'd wanted him to stay and convince her his feelings were true.

"I guess…" Cate set down her empty plate

and studied her fingernails, barely resisting the urge to slip her thumbnail between her teeth. She'd been doing so well on breaking that habit. She shoved her hands beneath her legs and glanced to Luc, who was patiently waiting for her to continue. Analyzing her intently in that unnerving way he had. "I suppose you're right. It was easier to be upset with you for what happened at the end—"

Luc growled. "I never so much as laid eyes on another woman, Cate, if that's what you're referring to."

What did he want her to say? *Suddenly, I believe you*? Cate had fallen so hard and fast for Luc when they were young that when the question of trusting him had arisen, she didn't have an answer. How did a person go about choosing to put their faith in someone? How did that work? And what if they made the wrong choice? Cate's trust button was broken, and she didn't know of a repair shop that worked on that kind of issue.

Except for God. But He hadn't healed that gaping wound in her life. At least not yet.

"Let me finish. It was easier to be mad at you for how things ended than it was to be upset at myself for doing what I did to you. Easier to blame you than to admit it was fully my decision to keep Ruby from you. Because if I could focus on what I saw as your part in all of it, I didn't feel as guilty."

Ouch. Cate had never admitted anything of the sort to herself. She'd just been pointing fingers. Deep down, she'd known it was wrong not to tell Luc about Ruby, but she'd been so afraid of losing her daughter that she'd let that keep her from doing the right thing.

What a mess she'd made.

Luc was right. It wasn't just her and Ruby anymore. Luc was part of the picture. And she needed to stop treating him like he was an intruder and start treating him like Ruby's father.

No matter how painful the change.

* * *

This was the most truthful Cate had been with him yet. Luc wasn't sure if it was the brownie or the calm conversation that had her defenses down, but he liked this side of her. Then again, maybe it was dangerous to have Cate open up like this, because it flooded him with memories of what they'd had when they were younger.

Before she'd stopped believing him.

When they'd had that last fight—when she'd asked him for the truth—Luc had told her he'd never cheated in any way, shape or form. But when she'd pushed him, needing more information that he didn't have to give, he'd snapped.

Nothing messed with him like when people didn't take him at his word. It had happened in high school. A group of teens had vandalized the school. Yes, his buddies had been involved. No, he hadn't been. Yet, somehow, even his own parents hadn't believed him. Luc had looked them straight in the eyes and told them the truth—that he'd been at home in bed. He could understand the story sounding fake, but it hadn't been. But they'd trusted someone on the school staff—an eyewitness who placed him at the scene of the vandalism—instead of him. And he'd been forced to do community service with the guys who had caused trouble.

Ever since then, not being believed was his greatest aggravation. When Cate had done the same thing to him, despite him telling her nothing but the truth, something in him had hardened. Cracked and bled.

He'd been done. That was why he'd run and never let himself look back, though the temptation had been strong to call Cate the morning after they'd fought. To make everything right again.

But it hadn't been any old argument. Not to him.

Not one part of Luc had wanted to walk away from Cate, but he'd made himself.

How could they have continued a relationship when she didn't trust him?

Bruised and limping, he'd gone back to the ranch. Soon after, his parents had needed to move for his mom's health, and he and his sisters had taken over.

And he'd been fine. For the most part. Until Cate had shown up with Ruby.

But now he couldn't avoid Cate's lack of trust. They had Ruby, and they had to deal with each other. The question was, how? Today showed that the way they'd been functioning wasn't working.

Cate hopped down from the kitchen counter that held them both, and Luc's breath hitched. Was she going to take off? End their conversation? Because he wasn't done yet.

She grabbed her plate, then his, heading for the industrial sink.

His shoulders relaxed. "I'll do that."

She waved one hand, her back to him. "Strangely enough, I like washing dishes."

"I'm not going to argue with that." He

didn't know if she smiled or not, and curiosity inched along his spine. It was easier when he could read her. If he could manage to.

She pulled down the sprayer and squeezed the handle, the water making a zinging noise as it hit the dishes and stainless-steel sink.

"Cate, we have to figure out how to get along." The water momentarily stopped. "For Ruby's sake." Back visibly unknotting, she went back to cleaning—squirting dish soap and using the sponge resting near the edge of the sink. "I want you to let me into your lives. It doesn't work for our relationship to be just about Ruby. I mean, yes, that's the focus, but we can't hold each other back with steel rods. She'll figure out soon enough that we can't get along. It won't work. Not in the long haul. We have to parent together."

It was almost easier to talk to Cate with her back turned. But at the same time, he'd give good money to see her face. During his speech, she'd continued scrubbing one of the little plates as if it was covered in hardened cement she needed to scrape free. Finally, she put both plates in the metal drying rack to the side of the sink and turned to face him.

"So what are you saying?"

"I'm saying I want in. I want permission to have Ruby, to let her go off with Emma or Mackenzie or me without thinking you're going to come after me with a pitchfork. I want the chance to be her dad and have the responsibility and freedom that comes with it. And I'd like us to be on the same team."

Luc held his breath while Cate processed, letting it out in a gush of air when she outlasted him.

She lifted her thumbnail to her mouth, then ripped it back out. "Okay. I hear you, and you're right. I have been holding you back. So I'll stop, and we'll parent together." A flash of pain crossed her face, followed by a look of determination. "We can manage that, can't we?"

Luc pushed off the counter and stood. "I think we can."

Doubt and concern swirled in her pretty brown eyes, and he resisted the urge to reach out, tuck her into his chest and just hold on. Would it heal something between them if he breached the gap of hurt that separated them?

If only it were that simple.

Cate slid the brownie tray back into its spot on the shelf, and Luc dried their plates and put them away. They faced each other again, both leaning against a counter.

A lock of hair tumbled across Cate's face, and she tucked it behind her ear. "So, does this mean I get to make all of the decisions, and as long as I talk to you about them first, you have to agree?"

"No." Funny girl. "If anything, it should be the other way around."

Her nose wrinkled. "I don't really see that happening."

"I don't, either." A chuckle vibrated his chest. He'd take humor over fighting any day.

They walked through the dining room and into the lobby area of the lodge. Luc had always found it a comforting place. Large, overstuffed leather couches and chairs. A fire burning on cool evenings.

Cate paused by the front door. "I meant to tell you Ruby's day care called, and they're going to refund part of the month. They found someone who needed a temporary spot while they're on a waiting list. I know you said you'd pay for it in order for her to be here, but now you don't have to. It's nice. Between that and the meals being provided, I'm actually saving money." She looked surprised by her own admission.

"Good. I'm glad to hear it." He still didn't know how Cate had scraped by as a single mom. She must have worked incredibly hard to stay afloat. "There's something I've been meaning to tell you, too."

She waited for him to continue, but nerves got tangled up, congregating in his throat. What in the world? It was just Cate he was talking to. Just the mother of his child. First and only woman he'd ever loved. He didn't need to be so skittish around her. But she messed with him in a way no one else did.

Plus, he didn't think she'd take what he had to say very well.

"I have some money set aside, and I want you to have it."

Confusion wrinkled her normally smooth complexion. She blinked. "For what?"

"For Ruby. For you. All of this time you've raised her on your own without any help. That's not right. I would have—" He clamped his jaw shut to keep from saying he would have been there for Ruby and supported her. It was true, but now that they'd both declared a truce, Luc didn't want to cause a rift in the new peace they'd found.

He might never fully understand the choice Cate had made, but he had to find a way to move beyond it. For all of their sakes.

"I want to help out. I want to be part of taking care of her. So I *am* going to give you what I have." He wished it could be more, but while he lived comfortably and contentedly, he wasn't a millionaire by any means.

They'd have to figure out better logistics going forward, but he wasn't ready to deal with the thought of Ruby and Cate leaving the ranch at the end of the month.

"I didn't find you because I was looking for money." She searched his face as if scavenging for the meaning behind his offer.

"I know."

"Ruby and I have always done okay."

"I'm not saying you haven't. But are you telling me there's not a pile of medical bills filling your mailbox? Or that there won't be shortly?"

The scuffed wood floor beneath their feet caught and held Cate's attention.

Luc gently nudged her chin up so their eyes met. "Give me this, at least. Let me do this." Then it would feel like he was doing *something*. Cate made mothering look so easy, Luc feared she really didn't need him. And the past few years had proved she didn't.

A group of guests walked by the front door, the hum of their conversation trickling into the lodge.

"Well?" he questioned when their voices faded.

Her hands momentarily rose in defeat. "I want to say no, but I don't think you're going to let me."

"I'm not."

She waited one beat. Two. Three. A faint smile sprouted. "Okay, Lucas. You win."

When she looked at him that way—with softness instead of a crisp outer shell, his full name falling from her mouth like silk— Luc couldn't help feeling like he *had* just won. It was the first time he truly had hope that a second chance—for their daughter—was an actual possibility.

Chapter Eight

"Daddy, watch!" Ruby held on to the back of Molly, the ranch's black Lab, and squeezed for all she was worth. Thankfully, Molly had the sweetest temperament of any dog on planet Earth and barely blinked an eye. "Molly likes to give me huggles."

"That's great. Good job." Luc wasn't sure whether he was saying it to his daughter or the dog.

The Saturday afternoon sun beat down on them, and Luc removed his hat and swiped his brow before plunking it back on his head. He should probably throw some sunscreen on Ruby, though they'd only been outside the lodge for a few minutes.

Cate had trained him to apply the stuff whenever there was even the slightest chance the sun would come into contact with Ruby's fair skin. As a kid, Luc hadn't thought twice about sunscreen. And he'd spent as much of his childhood as possible outdoors. Had they even made it back then? He recalled his sister Emma using baby oil to gain a tan. That had not ended well.

"Sit, Molly." Ruby wagged a finger, and Molly's rump hit the ground. The dog gave Luc a look as if to say, *How long do I have to do this? I'd better get a treat.*

Molly knew exactly where the dog bones were kept—in an old metal milk can on the front porch of the lodge—and if Luc wasn't mistaken, she was repeatedly stealing glances in that direction.

"I did it." Ruby's hands flew into the air in celebration, as if Molly had never performed a trick before in her life.

"See if you can get her to roll over. You can get her a treat."

Ruby clapped in excitement, and Molly's soft ears perked with interest. Fast as her little legs could go, Ruby ran onto the porch, uncovered the bin and snagged a bone. She ran back to Molly just as Joe pulled up to the front steps with a pickup full of food.

The small grocery store in town ordered some of their supplies so the money could stay local. Joe or one of the kitchen staff usually picked up a load after the guests left on Saturday mornings. What they couldn't supply was delivered by refrigerated truck.

Luc popped the tailgate down as Joe eased out of the truck slowly, nursing his bad hip. Pulling a handkerchief from his pocket, he swiped the beads of sweat from his midnight forehead.

"Thanks for the help." He nodded at Luc. "Guess I have to forgive you for stealing brownies from my pan. Just like when you were a kid." Joe punctuated the sentence with a rumbling chuckle. He might talk big, but no one actually believed his threats.

Dad had hired Joe when Luc was a boy, and he'd been a part of their extended ranch family ever since.

"Does that mean I should just ignore the fact that you've been sneaking my daughter treats? How do you think her mother would feel about that?"

Not happy. Cate had rules about the number of desserts Ruby could have in a day. But Molly wasn't the only one who knew where to find treats. Ruby had quickly figured out the head chef had a soft spot for her, and she'd happily taken advantage.

Joe harrumphed. "Don't know what you're talking about."

Luc laughed.

The man attempted to straighten the fingers of his left hand, but arthritis had locked them into a painful-looking position. Well into his sixties, he was unwilling to give up his job. Said it kept him going. But the body didn't always agree with the mind. Joe had assistants in the kitchen for all of his chopping and food prep, but Luc wasn't sure if he actually used them or if he still did that kind of painful detail work himself. Joe had been born without an off switch.

"I'll get this." Luc nodded toward the truck. "Your arthritis will be killing you if you carry any of this."

Joe looked like he was about to argue, but finally nodded. "Thanks. Appreciate it." He ambled up the stairs and disappeared into the lodge as Mackenzie bounded down the steps.

"Need some help?"

"Sure. Thanks."

She hopped up into the truck bed and slid items toward the tailgate. She was dressed in black shorts and a bright green tank with flip-flops on her feet, and her legs had earned a tan over the summer. Cate would have to talk to her about sunscreen.

"Must be nice sitting around in the sun all day," Luc quipped.

Mackenzie did a lot more than trail rides and rafting expeditions—helping manage staff and reservations, too—but he couldn't pass up the jab.

"Must be nice sitting in an air-conditioned office all day."

She knew he liked that part of his job the least. "I don't see you offering to do the bookwork. Anytime you want to take over, you just let me know."

Her nose wrinkled with disgust as if he'd offered her a pretty pink bow to wear in her hair. "Never mind. I take it all back."

With a hand on the side of the truck bed, she hopped back down to the ground while Ruby called out, "Aunt Kenzie, watch!"

Mackenzie paused, facing Ruby while shading her eyes with her hand.

Ruby had commandeered Molly into playing dead. Or just wore her out so much that she'd dropped down for a nap.

"Nice!" Mackenzie gave Ruby a thumbs-up.

Ruby started running in wide circles, encouraging the dog to follow her.

"She sure has a lot of energy for a girl who just had heart surgery. I remember when we were kids. Before you had surgery, I could always beat you in a race. But after? You left me in the dust."

"And have ever since."

Mackenzie punched him on the arm. It stung more than Luc would ever admit. His sister was one of the toughest people he knew—male or female.

Luc watched Ruby run and giggle, creator and only participant in her game. "Isn't it crazy to think that she just had a heart procedure? I mean look at her..."

"Yeah. She's pretty amazing." Mackenzie lifted a box into her arms. "You ever think about the fact that if she hadn't needed the hole fixed, Cate might not have been guilted into telling you about her?"

"No." His answer came out fast, and her eyes narrowed.

The two of them had always shared a strong connection. Luc knew when there was a pea under her mattress, and she knew when something was off with him.

Back when he'd escaped the ranch at nineteen, thinking he needed a different life, Mackenzie had been irate.

And when he'd returned home as the prodigal brother, she'd accepted him without question.

"Liar." Mackenzie flashed bright white teeth. "Not that it's on the same subject or anything, but where's Cate?"

Luc shook his head. "You know I asked you to work on forgiving her. For Ruby's sake. And don't you dare say anything bad about her in front of—" He nodded toward Ruby.

"I wouldn't do that." Mackenzie had the

decency to look chagrined. But it only lasted a moment. "Have *you* forgiven her?"

"I'm working hard on it." And that was the truth. "In answer to your question, Cate has a deadline today for some magazine she does. She's been at it all week." Luc hadn't seen much of her at all—Cate had barely looked away from her computer for days. He'd even brought her a dinner plate last night because she'd sent Ruby with him and never come to get any food for herself.

Luc didn't know how she did it. He might very well die if he was strapped to a screen as much as Cate was. But she did look cute in those glasses she wore while working.

Because she'd been so wrapped up in work, Luc had gotten to spend a lot of time with Ruby this week. He'd been latching on to every minute. After their talk on Monday, Cate had been much better with him taking Ruby. And he'd been better about communicating. Look at them. They were practically getting along. If you didn't count the fact that they'd hardly seen each other.

"Well, the woman's not lazy. I'll give her that." And with that generous announcement, Mackenzie headed into the lodge with a box full of supplies.

Cate's everything hurt. Sitting in a chair for five days straight had taken a toll on her body. But she was finally done and could send the magazine off.

Her deadline had approached too quickly yesterday, so she'd asked for an extension until today at five. Thankfully, they were fine with her request.

And…she glanced at the clock on her computer screen…she'd be sending it in at quarter till. Nothing like beating a deadline with time to spare.

She wasn't usually so behind with the magazine, but with the time spent not working during Ruby's procedure and then redoing Vincent's project, she'd gotten off schedule.

A knock sounded just as she hit Send on the email, and Luc's hello followed, echoing into the cabin through the walls. Cate popped up, tossed her glasses onto the desk and hurried to let him and Ruby in.

Luc had pretty much taken care of Ruby all week while Cate worked. Whether their daughter had hung out with Luc or his sisters each day, she wasn't sure. A little of both, according to the stories Ruby told when she came back to the cabin exhausted and happy at night.

A quick bath and she fell asleep faster than Cate had ever seen her do before. All of that fresh air and dirt under her fingernails must be wearing her out.

Cate yanked open the door, only thinking about her appearance when it was too late. Luc's chin dropped. And not in a *whoa-woman-you-look-good* kind of way. This was more of a *what-happened-to-you* glance.

"Hi, Mom." Ruby waltzed into the cabin while Cate's hand snaked up to gauge the hair situation she had going on. Messy bun. Heavy on the messy part. Light on the bun. More of a hair band barely holding on to its dignity.

And her clothes. Cate's gaze bounced from Luc's black T-shirt, jeans and boots to her own yoga capris and pink T-shirt. The chipped toe polish on her bare feet looked as if it had been attacked by pecking birds. What in the world? Had she gone into some kind of hibernation for the past month?

"I—" She swept a hand down her outfit. "Deadline day." As if that explained it all.

Luc was smart enough not to say anything to that. "If you need more time, I can keep Ruby longer."

"Oh, no." She motioned toward the bedroom. As if he could somehow read her mind and know she was pointing through the wall at her computer. Boy, she really was a hot mess at the moment. "I just sent it in, actually."

His face lit up. "Good. I'm glad. Maybe

now you can eat and sleep again." Thankfully, he didn't add *and shower*. Though Cate did in her own mind.

Luc's head tilted, gears turning in that way-too-handsome noggin of his. "We should celebrate."

Cate planned to. With a bubble bath and sleep.

"Let's go to dinner. The three of us. You could use a night out." He glanced toward her bedroom. "Or just a night away from a screen. With other people." He pointed his thumb at himself, as if she didn't remember what the concept meant.

Dinner with Luc sounded like all sorts of trouble.

"It would be good for Ruby to see us getting along."

Low blow.

"Believe it or not, there's a Thai restaurant that opened up in town not too long ago."

Her mouth watered. How did he remember she loved Thai food? Then again, she knew he couldn't stand the texture of shredded coconut, that his skin reacted when his clothes were washed in bleach and that he liked his tea unsweetened.

"And don't give me some lame excuse about your outfit. You could wear what you have on and no one would be able to keep their eyes off you."

Like an ice cube tossed into boiling water, her disobedient body melted. "I really need to shower."

"Okay. I'll swing by with the truck and get you and Ruby. An hour?"

If only her head didn't nod in response when it really, really needed to shake in the other direction. The one that said no and kept a distance between them. But she'd promised Luc she'd work on doing the opposite of that. For Ruby's sake.

She shut the door on Luc's retreating back and turned. "Ruby, let's get ready. We're going out to dinner."

The little squeal of excitement that followed was most certainly not echoed within the walls of Cate's chest. At least not out loud.

Usually she didn't celebrate the small things in life like a deadline that came around once a quarter. There just wasn't time. And she didn't have the energy. But it was a nice idea. And Luc was right—she did need to get out of the cabin.

It was just…she hadn't had anyone to celebrate with in a really long time. Pretty much since Luc.

And if that wasn't a dangerous thought, she didn't know what was.

Chapter Nine

Just because Luc had showered and changed into crisp jeans, camel laced boots and a short-sleeved plaid button-down didn't mean tonight equaled a date. At least that was what Cate kept telling herself.

Luc parked the truck in one of the spots in the small lot next door to Thai House. The restaurant sign was newly painted, pink letters popping against a white backdrop.

Before Cate realized what was happening, he was on her side of the vehicle, opening her door.

Still not a date.

"Mommy," Ruby piped up from the back. "Let's go."

Impatience was easy to come by with a three-year-old, and Ruby had never been a fan of being strapped into her car seat.

Cate stepped out of the truck and into the warm summer evening, tossing Luc a hopefully breezy thank-you. One that wouldn't give away the pounding and banging happening within the confines of her rib cage. She wore a sleeveless navy-and-white-striped button-down, skinny ankle jeans and brown leather flats. Casual and comfortable, but not overly…date-ish.

Tonight's dinner didn't mean anything. And neither did the door. Luc was a gentleman. That couldn't be shaken out of him.

Luc released Ruby from her car seat, and she scrambled out as if headed to a parade. Perhaps they both needed some time away from the ranch. Not that Ruby hadn't fallen in love with it. She had. The lifestyle and guests had become part of her routine, and

Cate had no doubt she'd miss it all when it was time to head back to Denver in two weeks.

For dinner Ruby had changed into salmon capris and a teal shirt that boasted, *I got an A+ in talking.* A legitimate claim. From the reports that had filtered back to Cate this week, Ruby greeted anyone and everyone who stayed, worked at or so much as glanced in the direction of the ranch with her trademark, "Hi, friend."

According to Luc, anyone who came across her path was quickly smitten.

Rounding the side of the building, the three of them met up with the sidewalk. Westbend reminded Cate of a vintage postcard showcasing a small town from decades past. The kind one might find wrapped in protective plastic coating tucked into a bin in an antiques shop.

A ranch supply store anchored the corner, parking lot half-full of sale equipment. The main street was lined with small stores and restaurants, streetlights lit up in anticipation of evening.

They'd passed the quaint white church that Cate and Ruby had been attending with Luc and his sisters on their way to the restaurant. Cate had enjoyed the sermons, and Ruby had even gone to Sunday school. An easier transition than Cate had expected since they attended a mega church in Denver. So many people had welcomed her, wanting to get to know her.

Luc opened the glass restaurant door, exchanging the warm outdoors for a cool blast of garlic and lemongrass.

The bright orange sign just inside—also hand-painted—directed them to "seat yoself." The place was tiny, with a handful of tables and one long tabletop bar in the window, four metal stools lined beneath it.

Of course, Ruby wanted to sit by the window. A bit awkward for conversation since none of the seats faced each other. "How about a table instead? You can still choose," Cate added.

After two more attempts to pick the same spot, Ruby finally skipped over to a table on the far side with a cushioned bench lining the wall. She sat there with Luc, and Cate took the chair across from him.

Each table held a flickering candle in a brightly colored glass jar.

Still not a date.

The air-conditioning came in spurts of cool and then tepid air as the waitress dropped off waters and paper menus.

Luc left his untouched. "You're going to have to order for me." His grin made her stomach shimmy. How many times did she have to remind herself he was off-limits? *They* were off-limits.

Thai wasn't Luc's favorite, but over their time together, she'd found a couple of items he enjoyed. Good memories pressed in, more vivid than she'd allowed them to be in a long time.

"Mommy, what about me?"

One minute with Luc, and Cate had already forgotten about their daughter, perched on the bench next to him. Exactly why she and the man across from her were a huge *no*. The feeling of being forgotten was something Cate had carried with her from childhood to this day. Not one she wanted her daughter to experience.

"I'll order for you, sweets."

"Okay. I want the rice soup."

"Got it."

"She knows what she wants?" Luc asked. "What three-year-old eats Thai food?"

Cate's teeth pressed into her lip, biting back amusement. "She wasn't really given a choice. She grew up on it. If we ever eat out or grab something to go, which is rare… Thai is pretty much what we get."

"The first step is admitting you have an addiction, Cate."

She laughed. Luc's teasing just might be yummier than the food they were about to eat.

When the waitress came back, Cate ordered the soup for Ruby, a mild yellow chicken curry for Luc—it had potatoes in it, so he'd at least be able to recognize those—and pad thai for herself.

A small cup of crayons was on the table, and Ruby colored on the sheet the restaurant supplied. Her small tongue slipped between her lips as she concentrated.

"So," Luc said, "what do you think about living at the ranch?"

"I like it," Ruby piped in, adding a strip of red to her rainbow.

Since he'd been looking across the table at Cate, his question had obviously been meant for her. Their curving mouths mirrored each other's at Ruby's quick answer.

"Good." Luc captured Ruby in a hug. "Because I like you."

With a smile that said she deserved every compliment headed her way, Ruby wiggled with happiness, then went back to drawing.

Luc turned back to Cate, obviously waiting for her answer.

"It's not what I expected."

"What did you expect?"

"Actually, I have no idea." She laughed, and the skin around Luc's eyes crinkled in response.

"Everybody's happy," Ruby said.

"What?" Cate caught the yellow crayon as it rolled in her direction, sending it back across the table. "What do you mean?"

Ruby just shrugged and went back to drawing.

Trying to read a three-year-old's thoughts wasn't easy, but Cate had an inkling she knew what Ruby meant. Could she tell that her parents were getting along? That Cate had done her best to give up big chunks of control this week?

"Are you thinking what I'm thinking?" Luc lowered his voice. "That she's referring to us?"

"Kind of." Amazing that at her young age,

Ruby still had a finger on the pulse of their relationship. Luc had been right about that. "I guess she could tell when you were making things so difficult."

Luc gave an exaggerated snort and then laughed, and her insides warmed like molten chocolate cake. It was nice finding their friendship footing again. This dinner was making Cate think they could get along as parents without letting anything romantic bloom between them.

The door opened behind her, and Luc's face lit up with recognition. A woman? Cate resisted turning, though it was as hard as waiting for cookies to cool when they came out of the oven. Scalding jealousy closed off her throat, not boding well for the pep talk she'd just given herself about her and Luc being *just friends*.

Luc waved whoever it was over, and Cate gave a stern talking-to to her overactive ovaries, which obviously thought since they'd helped create this man's child, that they somehow still had a claim to him.

But it wasn't a young, beautiful female who appeared, like her imagination had quickly conjured, but a man instead.

Maybe late twenties? Broad build. He wore jeans and a checked button-up shirt, the sleeves rolled up at his wrists. He didn't carry the rugged air of a cowboy like Luc did. He was more…fashionable. If that made any sense. Like he was wearing all the right stuff and didn't quite fit the mold.

"Cate, this is Gage, a good friend of mine. He ranches not too far from us."

They exchanged greetings, recognition tickling Cate's senses. She'd seen Gage before. At church, if she remembered correctly.

"Sit with us." Luc motioned to the table.

"I can't. Thanks, though. I just had a meeting, and I'm picking up something to go. Have a few things I need to do at home."

Scrutiny washed over Cate. Luc was always studying her, but strangely enough, it usually made her feel protected. Known. With Gage the vibe was different. More... distrusting. Not that she could blame him. She had done a number on Luc.

"I didn't know you ate this weird stuff."

Gage laughed at Luc's jab. "Still got a little of Denver in me." They called out that his to-go order was ready, and Gage said good-bye. He left just as their food arrived.

Cate took a tentative bite of her meal, not expecting it to be...good. Not this far from the city. But she was dead wrong. It was every bit as mouthwatering as her favorite take-out place in Denver. Maybe better.

"Have I possibly seen Gage at church?"

"Yep. He goes to the same one as us."

"I thought I remembered him talking to Mackenzie. It made me wonder if maybe they were..."

Luc paused with a forkful of chicken hovering over his plate. "What?"

Could he seriously not infer the rest of her

thoughts from her statement? Men. "If they were interested in each other."

"Mackenzie?" Luc scoffed. "No way. Gage has been a mess since his wife took off on him. Now ex-wife. I don't think so. Plus, the two of them wouldn't be a fit. Gage would need someone…softer than Kenzie."

What kind of guy *could* handle a woman with so much raw power oozing from her? Perhaps another superhero? "Does Mackenzie ever date anyone?"

"She did when we were younger, but he left town and she hasn't really dated since." Luc paused. Scrunched his nose. "At least, not that I know of. I'm not even sure she'd tell me. Though I'd probably have a clue. She can't really hide anything from me. It just… doesn't work that way between us."

"Twin connection is really a thing, huh?"

"It is for us."

"So do you think she's not over this guy she dated when she was younger?"

Now Luc's face wrinkled with something

close to disgust. "I don't know. I don't really spend my days wondering about or analyzing my sister's love life. Either of them."

She laughed. Despite her original misgivings about saying yes to this outing, she was enjoying herself.

"Gage is a lawyer. Not many people start ranching later in life, but his uncle left him the land, and he moved there about a year and a half ago."

"Does he still practice law?"

"When he feels like it. He's done well with the ranch. Seems to like his new life."

"It's strange. I can tell he's kind, but at the same time, something's off. Melancholy or… I don't know what." She'd only met him for a minute, but Gage carried an obvious burden on his shoulders.

"That's the Nicole-effect." Luc finished his dish in record time—so he must not have hated it too much—swiping his mouth with his napkin. "Though come to think of it, I don't remember him being real happy before his ex-wife left, either."

Ruby and Luc started talking about one of the horses she'd befriended this week, and Cate half listened, her mind stuck on Luc's statement about Gage.

What had people said about her and Luc when they were together? Had they recognized happiness? Their relationship certainly had ups and downs, but at the core, Cate had been blissfully content.

The question she didn't have an answer to was whether Luc had felt the same.

Despite Cate's protest, Luc paid for dinner. They left the restaurant, the perfect nighttime temperature sliding along his skin. The evenings always cooled off in Colorado—one of the reasons he loved this blessed state.

"Want to walk a bit?" Luc nodded toward the five-and-dime store. "There's a counter full of candy—"

Ruby didn't allow him to finish. She

grabbed his hand, attempting to drag him down the sidewalk. Luc chuckled and scooped her up. "Hang on. Your parents aren't as fast as you."

Your parents. Was he allowed to lump himself and Cate together like that? Sure, they were Ruby's parents, but that didn't make them a "them."

Cate walked beside him, the faint hint of her sweet perfume teasing his senses. Had she spritzed it on for him? Not a chance. Cate wanted nothing to do with him outside of Ruby, but the schoolboy in him had to tamp down the attraction buried for far too long.

Her hair was down in loose waves. She'd worn makeup—not that she needed it—and it brought the focus to her eyes and lips. He glanced away, uncomfortableness spreading through his body. Or more like too much interest that wasn't allowed.

At the five-and-dime, Luc propped the door open, letting Ruby down to walk in with Cate. She beelined for the counter that held an assortment of candies and sucker sticks, moving back and forth in front of the options.

Cate plucked a pack of colorful, small, round chocolates from the display. "This is what I always picked out as a kid. It was my favorite."

He palmed a pack of Big League Chew. "This was mine. Thought it would make me good at baseball. Didn't work."

She laughed. "Can't be good at everything."

Kind, lovable Cate had come out to play tonight, and she was majorly weakening his resolve. If she kept this up, Luc couldn't be held accountable for his actions. Like kissing her until their painful history was a distant memory.

When Cate let her guard down, it was too easy to remember how good it had been. Too easy to forget how quickly she'd distrusted him.

"What are you thinking, Rubes?" Cate picked up a fruit-flavored package. "What about this?"

Their daughter's head shook, and Cate's eyes met his, amusement and exasperation playing tug-of-war. "She'll never decide without a time limit. We could be here all night."

Should he be concerned he was feeling fine with that option?

"One more minute, sweets. Then you need to choose."

Ruby finally picked out a watermelon sucker stick, and Luc paid for the three items, his and Cate's choices included. He thought she might try to argue—she was good at it when she wanted to be—but Cate just accepted the chocolate with a thank-you and a youthful grin.

He opened the watermelon stick for Ruby while Cate dug in her purse and then sprayed sanitizer on Ruby's hands. They walked back outside, meandering down the sidewalk as Ruby smacked on her sucker. Cate opened her chocolate and Luc dug into his gum. Not *quite* as good as he remembered from being a kid.

They reached the park on the west side of the street, and Ruby begged to stop and play. It wasn't much. Swings, monkey bars and a couple of slides, but at their yes—and Cate's condition that Ruby couldn't have her sucker while she played—she ran off.

Luc and Cate sat on the park bench facing the equipment, the setting sun reaching for the pine trees that lined the hills. A plastic baggie appeared from the amazing depths of Cate's bag, and she tucked the open end of Ruby's sucker inside so she could eat it later.

Her shoulder nudged into his. "Thank you for tonight. I needed it but didn't realize how much."

"That's what I'm here for. All-around good guy. Saving women from working too hard."

Her laughter went down as easy as jumping into the creek on a hot summer day.

"You know what I've always liked about you?"

"My devastatingly handsome looks?"

"No."

"Ouch, woman. Take a little time before you answer."

Her lips curved. "That you were okay with who you were. Didn't care what anyone thought. You always seemed so comfortable with yourself."

"Might have looked that way to you, but I left the ranch because I thought I needed to be somebody else and didn't want my life dictated to me. When I was away, I missed it and had a hard time admitting I'd been wrong. Then I met you and didn't want to leave you."

Luc could fill in Cate's next thoughts for her, because his were the same.

"But then I did leave."

She sighed. Twisted the package of chocolates closed. "I told you to."

"Yeah. Guess we were both part of that scenario."

"Guess we were." Cate set the chocolates between them as if erecting a barrier. "Luc, while Ruby and I are at the ranch, I really want us to stay focused on her. The two of us as a team. Like we discussed."

He must be inching into Cate's space. Making her uncomfortable with their friendship. It was so *her* to want everything tied up with a neat little bow. *You stay on your side of the line. I'll stay on mine.*

She liked her house and her life compartmentalized. Defined spaces. Luc understood it. He wanted the same thing when it came to Cate. Didn't want any of the boundaries blurred between them.

For once they agreed.

Luc still didn't understand why Cate had done things the way she had. Maybe he never would. But despite his pull toward her, nothing would ever work between them if Cate couldn't trust him. And while she'd changed over time just like he hopefully had, he didn't think that area of her life had undergone a major overhaul. Plus, Luc hadn't moved past what she'd done in keeping Ruby from him. He might be praying for a forgiving spirit, but that didn't mean it had instantly happened.

"I just think Ruby needs all of our focus on her. Having you in her life is a big change, and we need to be vigilant about helping her through all of this."

In his opinion, Ruby had adjusted lightning fast. Almost overnight. Accepting him as if she'd been watching and waiting for his arrival. Maybe she had been.

Even so, Cate didn't need to keep stating her case.

"I agree with you." Luc should be thankful they both felt the same way, but his gut sank to his boots.

Surprise flashed. "Really?"

"Of course. That's what these few weeks are all about. Getting to know Ruby. Making her comfortable with both of us in her life."

"Right." Cate nodded definitively and glanced away. Did he sense disappointment swirling from her direction? Doubtful. But if she did harbor at least a hint of remorse, that would make him feel better. Like he wasn't alone in fighting off the magnetized pull between them.

"Look at us. In agreement again." Luc stretched his arm across the back of the park bench, accidentally grazing Cate's shoulder as he did. "Who would have thought, huh?"

Her eyes danced, lips matching his grin. "Who would have thought?"

"Mom, Dad." Ruby paused at the top of the slide. "Watch me!" She flew down, popped up at the bottom and ran toward them. She pushed between their legs, happiness palpable.

"Daddy, can I go on the campout this week? I want to go really bad. Pretty, pretty please!"

Every Wednesday the ranch offered an overnight campout. It was a popular activity. Stars like most people had never seen before. They had tents for those who wanted them, but most chose to sleep near the fire.

Ruby had probably heard about it at Kids' Club.

Luc might be surprised by the request, but that didn't mean it wasn't possible. He wasn't the one running it, but they could still go. It would be a good memory for the two of them to have together. Growing up, he'd done it more times than he could count with his dad.

"I suppose we could—"

"Ruby," Cate interrupted. "Why don't you go swing for a minute while I talk to your dad about it?"

"Okay." Ruby skipped back to the equipment, her two twisted hair buns bouncing along with her.

"I thought we were parenting together," Cate snapped.

Had a cold front rolled in during the last minute? "We are. I was *going* to tell her that you and I could talk about it."

"Oh." She eased back against the bench, her exhalation uneven.

"But if she wants to go, I don't see why she can't. I'm happy to take her. I'll keep her safe and bring her back if anything goes wrong or she doesn't want to stay. There's no danger in it."

"No danger?" Large eyes landed on him, sparking with the first hints of orange sunset. "Sleeping in the middle of nowhere with mountain lions and snakes and bears and who knows what else? She's not even four years old!" The last sentence came out in short, angry bursts.

Luc moved his arm back to his lap, swallowing a bark of laughter at Cate's overactive imagination. As if the animals she mentioned were prowling around the campfire while everyone slept. But then exasperation ignited, quickly burning up the remaining oxygen in his lungs. Hadn't they already had this discussion?

"I thought you were actually letting me have a say in Ruby's life. Or was that just because you had a deadline and needed help? Was that all that was going on this week? I should have known better."

"That's not true." She crossed her arms, one hand pressing so tightly into the flesh of her biceps it caused the skin to turn white beneath her fingertips.

How long could they keep dancing to this song that never ended? "Cate, I promise, it's completely safe. If it wasn't, we wouldn't be able to do it with our guests every week. Our liability insurance would shoot through the roof if anything ever went wrong. But it doesn't. I'm not saying I can promise nothing will ever happen to her. Neither of us can do that, but I will take care of her."

"Watch me!" Ruby called from the swings. She pumped her legs, sending her sandals reaching for the sky.

They cheered her on, Luc welcoming the momentary interruption. "That's pretty amazing she can pump already. Did you teach her?"

"No. She figured it out at day care this summer. Luc, I just can't imagine why she needs to sleep outside or how that's a good idea in her condition."

And they were back at it. Cate was stuck in the rut of thinking of Ruby with a hole in her heart. But she wasn't that little girl anymore. "She doesn't have a heart condition now. It's fixed."

Memories of Luc's childhood flared to life like old VHS tapes. He'd had open-heart surgery at an older age, so he remembered quite a bit about that time. People tiptoeing around him. Rules and regulations. He'd always wanted to be doing what all the other kids were doing. And after recovering from surgery, that was exactly what he'd done. One night he'd heard his mom and dad discussing it, and he knew it had been hard on her. But she'd also learned to let go. Which, in his opinion, Cate definitely needed to do. Not that he could tell her that straight-out. He did *not* see that going well.

"She doesn't have to do the campout. But she wants to. I don't think it's a big deal, but you do. So what are we going to do about that?" *Let me guess. You're going to win.* Luc had never been more thankful for words to stay in his head and not leap out of his mouth.

"I don't know." Agitation radiated in the tense lines of Cate's body. "I've never had to do this before." She motioned between them. And he finally understood at least one of her reasons for keeping Ruby from him. So she could control everything. And now he was pushing all of those buttons, making her share parenting with him. She must hate every moment. Every time he had an opinion meant she didn't get her way.

"Since we can't agree, maybe we let the doctor decide?"

An impartial mediator. He resisted rolling his eyes. Did they really have to go that route? Overkill, in his opinion. But what other choice did they have? The two of them weren't going to agree on a decision. "Fine."

A chill followed the conversation, the warmth resonating between them only minutes before dropping by the tens, and not just because the sun had slipped behind the hills. Would have been smart of Luc not to expect massive changes in one week's time.

And in case any romantic thoughts of Cate fought for air, Luc would snuff them out with the heel of his boot.

Because she definitely didn't trust him yet.

Chapter Ten

"Don't forget your toothbrush," Cate called to Ruby on Wednesday evening.

Ruby popped into the cabin bathroom, her excitement over the campout causing her to skip and gladly comply with everything Cate asked of her.

Where exactly would her three-year-old be brushing her teeth in the middle of the woods? Three! If Ruby could hear her thoughts, she would quickly call out, *Almost four!* Either way, she was far too young for this. Cate's head shook, though no one was present to witness her strife.

She'd never camped growing up. That hadn't been high on her family's priority list. She wasn't sure what to send with Ruby, so she'd asked Luc for a list. It was surprisingly short.

On Monday Cate had called the doctor's office. She'd expected them to voice concern. To ask questions. But the nurse she'd spoken to had seemed surprised Cate had called at all. She'd gotten the all clear for Ruby to go on the campout that not one part of her had been wanting.

If only they'd said no. Then Cate wouldn't have had to tell Luc he was right. And her daughter wouldn't be about to spend the night outside in the mountains.

Cate hated being the not-cool parent. The overprotective mama bear. This whole co-parenting thing had her scrambling to figure out how to fit together the puzzle pieces of their new life. And to make matters worse, when she'd told Luc, instead of rubbing it in that she'd been wrong to worry and call the doctor, he'd just thanked her for making sure it was okay for Ruby.

The old Luc had been a fighter. Not one to back down easily. But God had changed him. Made it hard for Cate to keep her eyes on the prize—Ruby—and not on the man who kept stealing her attention despite her best efforts not to let that happen.

Ruby bounded over to Cate, handing off the toothbrush. Cate added it to her pink backpack just as a knock sounded at their cabin door.

"Come in," she called out, and Luc let himself in. A snarl came from the kitchen sink—a place Prim would never occupy back in their apartment. Cate was starting to think the cat could sense when Luc might be arriving, because that was the only time she'd crouch in that particular hiding place. It was almost as if she wanted to torment Luc. Cate was trying desperately not to find it funny when Prim surprised him. So far she'd failed miserably at that attempt.

"Good to see you, too, Prim." Luc's dry tone earned a giggle and an enthusiastic hug from Ruby.

Currently, Cate sided with Prim. She was as excited to see Luc as she would be to run smack-dab into a hornet's nest. Because while he was starring as the picture of maturity, she'd taken the lead role as big ol' baby. And had learned over the past few days, unfortunately, that she excelled at the part.

"Cate?" Luc stood in front of her, too close for comfort, the questioning pucker of his brow telling her it wasn't the first time he'd said her name. She was falling to pieces—trampled wildflowers plowed over by horse hooves—and Luc smelled like a forest and looked as tall and strong as a one-hundred-year-old pine.

Jerk.

"Nothing is going to go wrong." His hands landed on her shoulders, the dueling colors of his hazel eyes leaning more toward hickory in the early evening light. "Ruby will be fine. We have emergency measures in place for the guests on a normal week. We can use them, but we won't need to. If she wants to come home, I'll bring her back no matter what time it is. The campout is simple. We'll ride up to the campsite. Tell stories, sing songs. Then we'll sleep on the hard ground and love it while you sleep in a pillow-soft bed. Ruby will be back in the morning and might even need a nap tomorrow."

Why was he being so nice to her? Cate would almost prefer feisty Luc. Then she could reach for anger instead of having to deal with her real emotions. Those were much harder to process. Concern and fear and maybe even a little dread all rolled together. With a sprinkle of loneliness on top. Ruby had never spent a night away from Cate.

Or maybe the bigger problem was that Cate had never been away from Ruby for a night.

"I'm not going to convince you about this, am I?"

Her head swung back and forth.

Luc's hands dropped to his sides. "Then I'm going to quit trying. You can come with us, you know. The offer still stands."

Cate had considered it, but one, she really didn't want to sleep on the ground, and two, she should be able to let her daughter spend a night camping out with her father. She had to practice letting go. Had to. "Thanks, but I'm good staying here. You two have fun."

"Okay, then, off we go. Rube-i-cube, give your mom a hug."

Ruby bounded over to her, and Cate held on until she squirmed to be released. Then Ruby ran out the front door, singing a made-up song about fires and stars and sleeping bags. She didn't seem *quite* as broken up about the whole thing as Cate.

"Her sleeping bag's by the door." Cate handed him Ruby's backpack and pointed to the pink sleeping bag, which would likely come back needing a good scrub. The one that Ruby had begged to include when they'd packed for the ranch. Cate had acquiesced, thinking it silly but not wanting to battle over something so small. And yet now here she was using it.

Luc snagged the bundle, and unexpected humor surfaced at the sight of such a rugged man holding so much pink.

"What caused that smile?" Luc glanced down, then back up, a full-fledged grin igniting. "I look good, huh?" He turned his chin to the side and struck a pose with supermodel flair.

She laughed. "You look funny." And heart-stopping. She wasn't going to tell him what she really thought. That watching him be a fantastic dad to Ruby was an attractive thing. That he was so good with their daughter that sometimes it made Cate ache all over—like a what-might-have-been flu.

"I'm going to assume by 'funny' you mean incredibly handsome."

"I'm going to assume you meant it when you said you'd bring her back if she freaks out. She's so little, Lucas."

Lucas. She'd always used his full name when she meant business. Recognition of that flashed in his eyes. They held on to hers, all kinds of emotion flooding the space between them.

"I promise. I'll take good care of her."

And then he was out the door and gone.

Luc probably thought that last statement was what had her so upset. So agitated. And absolutely, Ruby's safety was her highest concern. But running a close second was the thought of someone else taking care of Ruby. And doing a good job of it. Cate not being needed.

And therein lay the true problem. From the moment Luc entered their lives, Cate had begun losing Ruby bit by bit. And tonight another chunk of their relationship was being torn away. Built into something new.

Prim jumped down to the floor and sat

at Cate's feet, her look questioning. Tears formed as Cate scooped her up, rubbing a hand along her spine.

"He doesn't understand."

Prim's head angled to one side as if to say, *Then why don't you tell him?*

Not only was Cate talking to her pet, she was imagining the animal—or her conscience—answering her. A habit she didn't want to admit was commonplace.

Cate deposited Prim on the floor, and the cat immediately went to lie down in the patch of remaining sunlight by the back window.

"We have a night to ourselves. What should we do, Prim?"

Strangely enough, no answer.

Cate had just finished a big deadline, but more work awaited. Always. She could use the alone time tonight to get ahead. And if she focused on a project, then maybe she wouldn't be consumed by the image of Ruby sleeping out in the open with mountain lions prowling about, their golden-green eyes glowing in the darkness.

A knock sounded. Could something be wrong already? Cate hurried to answer, practically ripping the door off the hinges with her herculean effort.

Emma stood on the step, holding the screen door open. "Hey, what are you doing tonight? I was thinking about making a frozen pizza and watching a chick flick. And I know Luc's taking Ruby on the campout." Her free hand rested on the hip of her peach shorts that were paired with a simple gray T-shirt. When she worked with the kids and horses, Emma wore jeans and boots, but otherwise, she was often casual in cutoffs and flip-flops. "No pressure if you just want a night to yourself. I know you never get that, either."

Warmth cocooned Cate at the unexpected offer. "Can you do that? Make a pizza and not eat with the remaining guests in the dining hall?"

"Yep." Emma beamed. "Dinner is covered. I'm not in charge tonight. You in?"

Cate looked toward the bedroom as if she could see her computer through the wall, waiting for her. She was always so responsible. Had to be. But with the money she'd saved eating here and not paying for day care, and the check from Luc, things weren't as tight for once. She could breathe. And maybe that was exactly what she needed to do. For once in her young life, work could wait.

"I'm in."

A charcoal backdrop, tips of pine trees reaching for the stars, a deep, full breath filling Luc's lungs with the taste of campfire and crisp mountain air...and best of all, his daughter right beside him.

It didn't get better than this.

They'd roasted marshmallows and sang along while the talented Kohl played his guitar. The kids had run around earlier, playing tag, chasing each other with giggles and flashlights until parents had started calling for them to snuggle into their sleeping bags.

Ruby had spent all of her energy and now sat beside him, eyes glazed as she watched the flames dance.

"Tired?"

Her head shook, fast and furious, denial at its best.

"I think maybe we should just rest in our sleeping bags. You don't have to sleep yet." Though he imagined she would conk out once her head hit the small travel pillow.

A sheen of moisture joined the orange reflecting in the brown pools of her eyes. Luc snuggled her onto his lap, and she sat back against his chest, facing the fire.

"You okay?"

She glanced across the fire to where the family of kiddos she'd been playing with were settling down for the night. "My friends had to go to sleep." Her *r* sound switched into a *w*, and Luc pressed down on a grin.

When she was tired, her words got groggy, too. "How come Mommy didn't come?"

A question Luc wouldn't mind the answer to. But he could guess. "I think she might not want to sleep outside on the hard ground. Isn't she a weirdo?"

Ruby giggled. Nodded and grew serious again. "I miss Mommy."

"If you need to go home, we can do that. You don't have to stay all night. There's nothing wrong with wanting your mom."

She twisted into his shoulder. Finally, she spoke. "No. I stay."

He tucked a finger under her chin, tipping her eyes up to meet his. He had to know she meant it. Not one part of him wanted her to do this if she was frightened. It wasn't worth it. They could come back and do it a different week or month or year.

"Are you sure? Because we can go home easily. It's not a big deal."

"Are you gonna sleep right by me?" Ruby's eyes were big and beautiful. So trusting. Their message stole the air from his lungs.

"Definitely." She might be asking about their current situation, but in Luc's mind, it was a lifetime commitment to be there for her wrapped up in that answer.

"Okay, good." Ruby climbed off his lap and into her sleeping bag, and though most of the adults weren't settling in yet, Luc took off his boots and zipped into his so he was near her.

Quiet voices and guitar strings created a lullaby with the crickets. It wasn't long before Ruby's lashes rested on her cheeks, casting shadows in the flickering light.

Beautiful girl. Inside and out. Luc stared up at the bright, endless stars, his mind full.

You missed so much of her life.

Yes, but Cate didn't have to tell me about her at all. And she did.

The two camps warred, agitation stealing his immense peace from only a moment before.

I don't want to do this anymore, God. I

don't want to live this way. I have to let go of the choice Cate made. Help me.

He'd been praying along those lines for weeks, but tonight he meant it. Luc could take either fork in the road in front of him, and he knew which one he didn't want: bitterness.

What would it have been like if Cate had told him about Ruby right away? He would never know the answer to that question. But he did realize things wouldn't have been perfect. His behavior and attitude at twenty years old would likely have equaled a pile of manure. Especially because he didn't have a moral compass back then to direct him. Now God was his guide.

Maybe it had all worked out for the best that he hadn't been a part of Ruby's life until this summer. Either way, there was nothing he could do about it now. And he was tired of holding on to self-righteous anger.

It was time to release all of it and move forward.

Under an expanse of sky that reminded

him just how great and infinite God's love was, his prayers were finally being answered. He was shedding scars and leaving smooth skin in their place.

Luc shifted to study Ruby's sleeping silhouette. *Me and your mom...we're going to be okay. The three of us will be just fine. No need to worry your pretty little head about anything other than what horse you want to ride this week. Or if you can teach Molly a new trick.*

She smiled while still in peaceful slumber. Dreaming of s'mores? Or something else? Luc had been surprised by how well she'd handled the evening so far. Ruby just...fit. With him. At the ranch. The campout. She was a part of the tapestry of this land.

He'd loved watching her play tonight. Her infectious joy. The sense of adventure and high spirits that permeated her life.

Cate had done a really good job raising her.

And for once he wasn't irritated at the thought.

Finally! Luc blinked back unexpected moisture and stifled the desire to give a loud, whooping cheer. The rest of the guests likely wouldn't appreciate him waking the children or understand his happy relief at how amazing this change in him felt.

In the morning Luc woke with the scent of smoke in his nostrils and he assumed hair and clothes, one particularly annoying rock biting into his lower back, one sweet girl curled up in the sleeping bag next to him. When Ruby had whimpered during the night—only once—he'd looped an arm over her bag and she'd snuggled into him. And then she'd gone right back to sleep.

Luc had stayed awake for a chunk of time to make sure she was okay, drifting off after realizing she was.

Now the smell of coffee tempted him to brave the crisp mountain air and snag a cup. One of the wranglers had brewed it and put out the pastries that would make for a simple breakfast before the ride back down. Then if the guests wanted to grab a full breakfast with some protein back at the lodge, they could. Not everyone participated in the campout, so Joe would still have a full meal set up and ready to go.

Ruby turned onto her back, eyelids still closed, and he leaned over, close to her ear. "You did it," he whispered.

Her eyes popped open, a mega grin overtaking her tiny face. "I was a big girl."

"You were a very big girl."

Luc wouldn't have minded taking Ruby home last night, but he couldn't deny he was proud of her for pulling through.

During the ride back to the ranch, Luc felt lighter than on the way up. As though he'd left something heavy and dark up on that hill. And he had, in a way. He'd finally buried the thought that he would have handled things better than Cate. That he would have done the right thing when she didn't. The truth was, he didn't have a clue what he would have done as the person he was back then.

"I'm a-cited to see Mommy." Ruby's version of *excited* was one of his favorite scrambled words she used. No one corrected her. In fact, he'd taken to using it himself at times.

Me, too. The thought shocked him, and his shoulders straightened in response.

"She'll be so happy to see you," he answered Ruby, mind jumbled.

He couldn't *want* to see Cate, could he? Couldn't have missed her like Ruby did. That had to be a misfire in his brain. One that didn't even need addressing. Besides the fact that he'd just reached the point of forgiveness with her, Cate wanted nothing to do with him outside of his role as Ruby's father. She'd made that very clear the night they'd had dinner and watched Ruby at the playground.

Their focus was to be on their daughter,

not them. And Luc agreed with her then and now.

So he needed to rein in his thoughts. They had absolutely no business getting so far off track.

Chapter Eleven

Cate opened the cabin door before Luc even had a chance to knock.

She scooped Ruby up as if she hadn't seen her for weeks, squeezing her tight. Luc set her things just inside the door. No doubt clean Cate would have everything put away in a matter of minutes after he left. She ran a tight ship.

Cate looked and smelled fresh from the shower, her hair still damp. She wore white shorts and an army-green sleeveless shirt today, her feet bare. Considering he and Ruby had slept in their clothes next to a campfire, Luc shouldn't even be allowed in the same room with something as pristine as the woman in front of him.

"So how was it?" She moved to the couch and sat, Ruby snuggled against her.

"It went great. She did amazing. One small moment of homesickness, but when I asked if she wanted to come back early, she said no. So we stayed." He stretched his arms behind him, trying to work out the pesky new kinks in his back. Luc had led the campout a number of times when he'd been in high school and didn't remember having any issues. Guess those days were over.

"What did you think, sweets?"

She's questioning Ruby, not you. He gave himself a stern warning, just in case any of his rampant thoughts hadn't shaken off him on the trail.

"It was so fun, Mommy. We ate marshmallows. Lots of 'em. I think I had ten."

An accusing look swung over Ruby's head, hitting Luc square between the eyes.

He raised his hands in defense. "It wasn't that many."

"And then we sang songs and somebody played the brown thingy."

"Guitar," Luc filled in.

"I'm so glad you're back." Cate ran her hand over Ruby's forehead in a comforting gesture Luc wouldn't mind experiencing himself.

"We should get you cleaned up. I'll start a bath for you."

"But I don't want a bath!" Ruby wailed at a volume too loud to come from such a small body. She'd thrown a hissy fit once or twice since she'd arrived at the ranch—mostly in attempts to get her own way—but nothing that sounded remotely like this.

"But you love baths. We'll get out all of your toys. I'll even get you some kitchen stuff to play with in the tub."

Despite Cate's soothing, the tornado-siren coming from Ruby increased in magnitude.

"Don't. Want. To." Ruby squirmed in Cate's arms, fighting to break free.

"Okay, okay, we can do a bath later. Calm down." Cate tried that forehead soothing thing again. Didn't work this time. Like trying to pet a writhing shark. "She's exhausted." Her eyes met Luc's, something close to blame residing there.

"I'm sorry."

"It's not your fault. This isn't the only time she's had a meltdown. They're more common than not when she's tired. You can go, if you need to."

And leave Cate to handle the temper tantrum on her own? No way. Luc crossed over to them. Without asking permission, he plucked Ruby from Cate's arms. Her body went stiff as a board. He held her against him anyway, her head near his shoulder. Though of course she didn't loosen a muscle to let it rest.

"We had a fun time, didn't we, Rubes? Let's not cry too much or your mom will never let you go again." He strode from one end of the small living room to the other, needing to do something. He had to prove to Cate—and himself—that she wasn't the only one who could handle a cry-fest. If Ruby would be going back and forth between them in the future, it mattered that he could take care of her if she flew off the handle. Luc kept talking, and eventually Ruby's cry quieted. He listed the fun things they'd done at the campout. He repeated himself and went in circles, likely wearing a path in the wood floor. Sometime during his verbal explosion, Ruby's head had drooped to his shoulder.

"Luc." Cate touched his arm, and the warmth stopped him in his tracks. "She's asleep." Cate motioned to Ruby's face, which Luc couldn't see because she was facing away from him. "Do you want to lay her in bed?"

He nodded. After depositing her on top of the bedspread, Luc covered her with an extra blanket. Ruby rolled over and snuggled in, her eyes remaining closed.

Only then did he allow himself a huge breath of relief. Amazing that she could still be so stinking lovable after a fit of those proportions. He grinned, head shaking, and walked back into the living room to find that Cate had taken over his pacing.

A mixture of exhaustion and frustration eased along his spine. Was she going to lose it on him? Technically, Ruby's meltdown was his fault. He'd taken her on the campout. He was the one who hadn't thought it would be a big deal.

The idea of slipping out of the cabin tempted him. He teetered with indecisiveness near the end of the couch, then walked around the coffee table and dropped to the cushions. If he was in trouble, he might as well get it over with.

"Guess I shouldn't have taken her."

Cate's arms crossed in a protective barrier. "It's not about that."

Then what had her so agitated? Was it something with work? Or another part of her life?

"What did you do last night?" Knowing Cate, she'd been glued to her computer screen all evening.

"Emma and I shared a pizza and watched a movie." She stopped at the back cabin window, staring out as if she'd caught a pair of squirrels dancing together.

"That's good." His little sister had the best heart. It always made him concerned that she'd get taken advantage of. She was missing the edges Mackenzie had. Ones that protected. He'd have to tell Emma thank you, though he knew she'd say she liked Cate and had hung out because she wanted to, not out of any sense of responsibility.

"So if it's not about Ruby's fit, and it's not something bad that happened last night, what has you so hot and bothered?"

Her head jerked in his direction. "Me? Nothing."

He attempted to cover his bark of laughter with a cough. She didn't react. Didn't say anything at all.

Luc pushed up from the couch and crossed over to her, stopping too close for comfort, hoping invading her space might snap her out of this daze. "I smell like a campfire."

She still faced the window, arms in a protective self-hug. "You're fine. You always smell a little like the outdoors."

Huh. Interesting. Curiosity wrangled his tongue. "Is that a good thing?"

Just when he didn't think he'd get an answer, she nodded. "It is. You wouldn't be you without it." That might be one of the nicer things she'd said to him.

Her eyes were glossy. Worn. Could she be sick?

"Did you sleep at all last night?"

"Off and on. Better than I expected to, actually."

"She really didn't cry like that at the campout, Cate. She was a little sad before bed.

I offered to take her home and she wanted to stay. She did great, if that's what you're worried about—"

"It's not!" Moisture escaped, cascading down her cheeks, forming a line like baby ducks following their mama.

What was he supposed to do? Leave? Stay? Was she mad at him?

She swiped the tears away quickly, but new ones kept appearing. "I'm not upset thinking that it didn't go well. I'm upset thinking that it did." Her wail was painful and oddly reminiscent of Ruby's. What in the world did that mean? He didn't have a clue, but he did hate seeing Cate like this. So he did the only thing he could think of. What he'd just done with their daughter.

He held her.

Just like Ruby, she stiffened. Not deterred, Luc tucked her against his chest and tightened his arms around her, communicating that he didn't plan to let go anytime soon. After a second of hesitation, her hands fisted his shirt, not to push him away, but more like she was holding on. She sobbed into his T-shirt while he cradled her, all the while thinking that if Cate wasn't losing half the moisture in her body in tears, this wouldn't be the worst place in the world to be.

Catherine Malory had survived being pregnant on her own and raising their daughter for three—almost four—years by herself. But all it took was a month of Luc back in her life for her to break down in a heap and use him as her crash pad.

And the worst part was she didn't want to tell him why.

Somewhere during her episode, Luc had started rubbing her back in a comforting circular motion. He felt good. All warm and strong. A tower the strongest gust of wind couldn't budge.

Only he was the problem. So how could she explain that to him?

Her tears had stopped spilling a few minutes ago. At this point Cate was just prolonging being tucked against Luc's chest. But who could blame her? It was nice in this little cocoon. Safe from the world and any troubles. From her feelings, which had bubbled up too fast for her to shove them down like she normally did.

After one deep breath—and secret inhalation of Luc's somehow still addictive scent—Cate forced herself to peel away from him. Her body complained at the rush of cool that replaced Luc's hold.

He grabbed the tissue box, offering it to her.

"Thanks." She took one, attempting to make less of a mess out of what was sure to be a red, splotchy face. "Sorry about all of that. And the souvenir." She pointed to his shirt, where she'd left a wet circle of tears behind like a drooling baby. Classy.

Luc glanced down, then shrugged. "It's okay." A grin played with his features. "If it wasn't for the crying part, I would have been just fine with the rest of it."

Heat inflamed her face at the implication of his words. Had he meant them? Would he take them back? She didn't want him to.

She'd missed being someone's person. Missed Luc and the way he'd always been such a support to her. Her biggest fan. But Cate couldn't afford to feel that way about him again. He was already taking over too much of her life in the form of Ruby. She couldn't let herself fall this time. Not when Ruby's happiness was at stake.

When her parents had attempted getting back together after the divorce and it hadn't worked, it had been even more painful than the first time for Cate. And she refused to do anything of the sort to Ruby.

"Do you want to talk about what's wrong?"

"No." Cate shook her head in double answer.

"Can you at least tell me what you meant

when you said you were upset the campout went well?"

He'd heard that? How was she going to explain?

Cate wanted to send Luc home. To buy herself a few days to regroup and sort out the emotions that had tumbled so out of control today. But if she did, things would stay the same, and she'd live in constant fear of losing Ruby. She couldn't continue functioning under the weight of this dread. It was killing her slowly.

She moved to the couch and sat. Luc followed, leaving a ruler length of space between them. How could he be too far away and too close all at the same time?

"I told you about my parents' divorce when I was a little girl."

Luc nodded.

"I shared pieces of it with you, but not all of it." He remained silent, but his eyes were on her in a way that told her he was listening. "During the divorce, things got rough.

They seemed to almost enjoy fighting each other. Neither wanted to give in. It didn't matter what was at stake—they both put up a fight. Even when it came to me."

Cate struggled to even out her breathing. She hated talking about this. "They couldn't agree on custody. Both of them bad-mouthed each other to me, trying to sway me to their side. It was awful. Finally, the judge asked me where I wanted to go. Who I wanted to live with." She plowed ahead, knowing if she quit talking she'd never find the courage to finish. "I was ten years old and they made me choose between them."

Luc blinked, a sheen of moisture evidence of his sympathy. "What did you do?" His voice was low, quiet and filled with pain that matched the stabbing in her chest.

"I picked both of them. How was I supposed to decide something like that? I went back and forth, and they shared custody. I didn't know what else to do. I wanted to please everybody and didn't realize until much later that I couldn't."

Luc covered the space between them, his jean-clad leg landing snug against her thigh as he snaked an arm out and tucked her into the nook of his shoulder. Despite her misgivings and the warning sirens blaring in her mind—products of all the *why she shouldn't be doing this* reasons she'd just rehashed—Cate didn't fight him. Just one more time she'd let it slide. Accept the comfort he offered. The future wouldn't be filled with moments like this, so was it so wrong to enjoy it? To let herself believe she didn't have to do life alone?

Besides, it would be easier to say this next part without looking at him.

"I don't want to fight with you over Ruby." She felt him tense and continued before she lost her nerve. "That's why I didn't tell you about her when I found out I was pregnant. Yes, it was our argument and the fact that you never contacted me again. But it was also my fear."

Cate straightened and met the questions written on Luc's face. "I didn't want to lose her, and I was petrified that we'd end up fighting. That we'd do to her what my parents did to me—focusing on each other and not on her. And now that we're here, and you two are bonding, I'm worried that when we leave to go back to Denver, you'll file for custody and we'll end up arguing over her. I *will* share her with you. I promise. We don't have to go through the court system. I know we can figure it out." Her voice dropped to a pleading whisper. "But please don't try to rip her away from me, because then we will end up like my parents. And I don't want to do that to Ruby. I don't want her to feel like I did as a kid. I was a rope in my parents' hands, constantly pulled in one direction and then the other. But I never felt loved. Noticed. If anything, their fighting made me feel completely alone."

She sat on her hands to keep from answering the call of her fingernails, which were begging for her to indulge in old habits. "Seeing that the campout went well... I mean, yes, she had a meltdown after, but she does that after any late night. It wasn't you. You handled her so well when you got back here. It's like I'm not needed. And that frightens me."

Could she leave one thought in her head instead of letting them all fall out at once? Luc was going to think she was nuts and then she really would lose Ruby.

Cate's shoulders rose and fell as she tried to calm her racing nerves. She'd just dumped a lot on Luc. Some she hadn't planned to say. What would he do with all of it?

Warm, soft empathy radiated from his handsome face, the scruff from last night a shadow against his cheeks and chin. "Cate, I'm sorry about your parents. They shouldn't have done that to you." He swallowed, Adam's apple bobbing. "I can't imagine you as such a young girl having to make a decision like that…" His head shook. "And Ruby needs you. Always. There's no doubt about that. Even I need you to parent with me. I can't do this alone. And we're not going to do what your folks did. We're not them. You're nothing like your selfish parents. And I'd like to think that I'm not, either."

"You're not. That's why I'm asking for this. I get that it's a little unorthodox, but I just—"

"This is what you need to feel safe. To know that Ruby is protected and loved."

She nodded.

"Of course I want Ruby in my life, but I wouldn't fight with you at her expense. We'll figure it out together. I would never try to take her from you."

Relief trickled through her limbs, relaxing cranky, tense muscles. "Even after what I did to you? Why not?" She wanted to slap herself for the question and the panic it ignited in her, but at the same time, she needed to know. Needed to get all of this out now so that she could finally be free of this anxiety.

"Because that wouldn't be good or healthy for her. I don't ever want her to doubt how much we love her. Plus... I've forgiven you."

"What? When?" Cate whispered, afraid she'd heard wrong. Afraid she'd heard right and she would be missing one of the strongest walls that stood between her and Luc. She wanted that barrier between them. To know that he'd never harbor feelings for her again. That he could never love her. Because if there was a chance he could again...how would she resist?

Cate couldn't let her heart make another botched attempt at something that would break it forever.

"It was actually at the campout. I've been praying about it since I found out Ruby was mine, but last night that stronghold finally broke free. You not telling me about her is over and done, and I want to move forward."

Surprise and disbelief registered at the

same time. "But I don't deserve your forgiveness." Not after what she'd done.

The skin around Luc's eyes crinkled. "That's exactly what grace is all about."

Cate had experienced mercy when she'd become a Christian and truly understood for the first time that God loved her, inside and out. The good and the bad. But never did she think that the human being who would show her that kind of forgiveness on earth would be Luc.

The idea of trusting him with Ruby and the impact he could have on all of their lives…it was still scary. But she was willing to take a step in that direction.

And that was a first for her.

Chapter Twelve

Luc was supposed to be working. Instead, he was fighting constant thoughts about Cate. Like, what was she doing right now? Was she thinking about him? And then there was his personal favorite: What would it be like to wrap her in his arms and steal a kiss?

Like he used to have permission to do. *Used to* being the key phrase Luc needed to pound through his thick skull.

Ever since their conversation last week when Cate had opened up to him about Ruby and her childhood—her reasons why she'd done what she'd done—he'd had a hard time concentrating on anything *but* her.

Cate telling him didn't have anything to do with their relationship—it had been about protecting Ruby—but it was getting harder for Luc to only focus on their daughter. He'd begun to think of himself, Cate and Ruby as a family. And of the two of them as permanent fixtures at the ranch.

Not his most brilliant idea since none of those were viable options. In two short days they would head back to Denver. Luc kept reminding himself that was a good thing. He and Cate were better as parents and friends. A large chunk of him wanted more…okay, all of him. But he still wasn't sure Cate fully trusted him—about what had happened between them in the past, or what could happen in the future.

And he wasn't going down that road if she couldn't. Because despite what she might think, he was trustworthy. And he wanted someone who knew that down to their bone marrow. Who harbored no doubts.

A knock sounded on Luc's office door, and Gage poked his head inside. "Hey."

"Hey, man." Luc leaned forward and propped elbows on the desk. "I needed an excuse to quit for the day and here you are."

"At your service." Gage dropped a wedge of papers on the desk. "Brought you something."

"What is it?"

"Info about petitioning for allocation of parental responsibilities. The woman I asked got back to me about a week ago, and I kept forgetting to drop these off for you. Sorry for the delay. Of course I'll help if you decide to file yourself."

Ice slithered through Luc's veins. He'd shelved the conversation he'd had with Gage about custody, forgetting they'd even talked about it. At the time he'd been furious and still in shock.

It would not be a good thing for Cate to

know about that initial exchange or these papers. Not after what she'd told him last week.

"I spaced that we'd even discussed this." Luc pushed the papers a few inches in Gage's direction as if they were a contagious disease, wanting to scrub his hands clean after touching them. Or use some of Cate's always-ready hand sanitizer. Like she made Ruby do after handling pretty much… anything. "I'm actually not going to file for custody. Cate and I are going to work things out between us."

Luc had gone over and over the same question in his mind since Cate had opened up to him: Could he trust Cate with his daughter? His gut said yes. And after prayer, that answer hadn't changed.

Gage's jaw slacked, and he rubbed a hand across it, confusion evident.

"I'm sorry your friend did all of that work and I'm not going to use it. I can pay for it. Hate to waste anyone's time."

Dropping to a seat on the futon, Gage

leaned forward, resting elbows on his knees. "I'm not worried about that. It's just…what changed your mind?"

"Cate."

"Did she tell you not to file? Because I don't think that's a good idea. You don't know what she'll do when she leaves here with Ruby, and—"

"I do know." Luc swallowed a rush of frustration. Gage was only trying to help. But sometimes the bitterness of what he'd been through with his ex-wife jaded his perception of the whole world. "We talked about it. We're going to work everything out. There's no need for paperwork or the court."

"But how can you just trust her?"

"Because I'm choosing to." And Luc wanted the same respect from her. He wished she would have trusted him when he'd denied seeing anyone else like she'd accused him of. Maybe they wouldn't be in this predicament now if she had. If there was anything he understood, it was the need to be believed.

"Does that seem like a good idea?"

"It's the one I'm sticking to." Luc didn't tell Gage about Cate's childhood. That was hers. Personal. He imagined it had been hard for her to share it with him, and he was thankful she had. Ever since their talk, he'd been much more at peace, knowing she would make sure Ruby stayed in his life, too.

"I'm sure you're silently calling me a cynic right now, but shouldn't you rethink this? As your lawyer—"

"You're not my lawyer. You're my friend."

"Okay, then, as your friend—"

Luc laughed. Shook his head. "There's no one I'd rather have in my corner than you." He picked up the papers and held them out to Gage. "But I don't need this info. And you're just going to have to be okay with that."

Gage groaned. "Fine. I'll let it go."

"Take these." Luc waved the stack.

"Keep 'em. Maybe something will change

in that hardheaded noggin of yours and you'll come around to the logical side again."

Luc dropped the incriminating evidence back to his desk with amusement.

The door opened without a warning knock, and Ruby flew into his office. "Daddy!"

He moved around the desk and swept her up. "Hey, Rube-i-cube." He squeezed her in a hug, the stress of the conversation with Gage quickly taking a hike. "Do you remember Daddy's friend Mr. Gage?"

Gage stood, greeting Ruby, asking her about her time at the ranch and receiving answers about how much she liked the horses and the people and even her bedroom. Luc's chest swelled with pride. She was such a sweet girl. Willing to talk to anyone. And the fact that she loved the ranch as much as he did didn't hurt, either.

"Ruby?" Cate's voice echoed down the hall, and Luc swallowed a flash of panic. The paperwork.

He sat on the edge of the desk, praying he covered the sheets. "We're in here."

Cate entered his office. "Sorry. I started talking to Emma, and Ruby just took off to find you." The woman was an irresistible bit of sunshine in a bright yellow shirt, navy capris and brown leather sandals.

He strangled the urge to stand up. "What are you girls up to?"

Cate's head tilted, confusion evident. "We came over to eat. It's dinnertime."

"Right." Luc glanced at the wooden clock on the wall. "Gage was here, and I lost track of time."

"Okay." Cate stretched out the *ay*, implying he wasn't doing a great job of acting normal. She greeted Gage, and the two of them chatted while he tried to figure out how to get Cate out of his office without her seeing the stack on his desk.

"Gage, you're welcome to stay for dinner," Luc offered. "It's rib night." And then the square dance would round out the evening.

Though thankfully Luc wasn't in charge of that. No one wanted to see his lack of rhythm on a dance floor.

"How can I say no to that?"

"Good. Glad you're staying, Gage." Cate quirked a thin eyebrow in Luc's direction. "Should we head to the dining room?"

He fought every instinct in his body screaming for him to push off the desk. He already felt awkward being the only one in the room *not* standing.

"After you." Luc lightly patted Ruby on the behind, and she grabbed Cate's hand, pulling her toward the door.

"Come on, Mommy. I'm hungry." Good girl.

He waited for Gage to follow, then quickly turned, shoving the papers his friend had delivered to the bottom of his to-do pile. Not a permanent fix, but it would get them out of sight for the moment. He'd have to come back later and shred the evidence.

He hurried to catch up with them, thanking the good Lord above Cate hadn't spied that information. The last thing he needed was to backtrack on all the progress they'd made and how far they'd come in their relationship. He wasn't sure they'd ever recover from what he'd once considered.

A small group lingered after devouring Joe's amazing fall-off-the-bone ribs, now sipping decaf coffee and overindulging in banana pudding cupcakes. Cate had quickly gotten used to the abundance of baked goods that came from Joe's skilled hands. Good thing she didn't have much longer to stay at the ranch, or she'd have to take up running or trailing after Mackenzie in order not to pack on extra pounds.

The hum of conversation around the table caused a sense of peace in her. Tonight's dinner had been easy. Even with Gage and Mackenzie. Were they warming up to her? Gage had been rather distant with her previously, but tonight he'd made more of an effort to engage her in conversation.

Cate couldn't shake the thought that she was fitting in with this crew. And liking it. Just as she and Ruby were gearing up to move back to Denver—they planned to pack up the car on Sunday—she'd found her footing.

But it was still good news for the future, because while she might not be living here, she would be involved in Luc's life and he in hers. That was what coparenting was all about.

If only the thought of being separated from Luc didn't smart like an art critique in college. Those days in school were the worst—her hard work up for everyone to criticize. She'd agonized over her projects for days beforehand and was currently fighting that same sense of dread.

But why? This was what she'd planned for all along. What she wanted. For her and Luc to be able to function as single parents who put their daughter's needs above their own. Wasn't it?

Luc's shoulder nudged hers. "You okay?"

His quiet question was for her ears only. Intimate. Goose bumps spread along her arms. "I'm good." Perhaps too much so.

But really, she should be the one asking him that question. He'd been jumpy in his office earlier. But at dinner he'd seemed fine.

Strange.

Ruby had finished her cupcake and now scooted around the table behind Luc, throwing her arms around his neck. He latched on, lifting her off the ground and causing a squeal of delight. In a split second he'd pulled her to his lap. She perched on her knees and held his face in her hands to procure his attention.

"Daddy, I want to go to the church thingy tomorrow night. There's going to be bouncy houses and games and cotton candy."

Cate vaguely recalled the pastor talking about the kickoff party for Wednesday night church clubs happening tomorrow evening—Saturday. But how had Ruby remembered?

"Sorry." Emma winced. "My fault. I'm taking my friend's boys tomorrow night, and we were talking about it." She motioned between her, Mackenzie and Gage.

Cate waved off Emma's concern, turning back to Ruby. "Sweets, we're not going to be here for Wednesday night church in the fall. Remember? We'll be back at our apartment in Denver by then."

Ruby's lower lip protruded. "I know, Mommy, but I want to go anyway. Pastor said everyone could go!" She must have been listening in church last week, too. Ruby picked up on more than Cate gave her credit for.

"I guess I don't mind. What do you think?" Cate asked Luc. "I can take her if you can't go."

"I don't have anything going on. I'm willing." Guests left on Saturday mornings, and

Luc usually took the day off after they were gone. At least he had since she and Ruby had been here.

"Yay!" Ruby jumped down from Luc's lap, spinning in circles of excitement behind them.

A night with just the three of them? It sounded...nice. Too nice. When it made her heart dance a jig with Ruby, Cate slammed the lid on her unacceptable reaction.

Those thoughts needed to remain tucked away, right where they belonged.

Tomorrow night would be a good way to end their time at the ranch and create a bridge to the next chapter in their story. To go back to the life she had with Ruby.

Messing everything up by allowing romantic thoughts about her and Luc to surface wasn't an option. Not when things were going so well between them.

It was just...ever since she'd confessed her fears to Luc, she'd been drawn to him like a bug to one of those zapper lights. A choice that could ultimately end in its demise. She kept trying to be logical and do what was best for Ruby. But the temptation to lean into Luc, to let herself inch in his direction, body and soul, was hard to fight.

A whiff of Luc's pine/grass/fresh mountain air scent spiraled her way, causing her to inhale slowly. To latch on to the small piece of him, knowing she couldn't keep him. But if things were different? If she could protect Ruby and have Luc? She'd let her head rest on his strong, capable shoulder. Slide her hand into his under the table like a teen not wanting to get caught.

If there was a different choice, she'd hold on to him and never let go.

It's not a date.

Once again Cate reminded herself that being out with Luc and Ruby did not a family make.

Even if she'd created a bit of trouble by wearing a red sundress with black wedges.

It was supposed to be casual. Fun and flirty. If Luc's smoldering eyes when he'd shown up at the cabin door to pick them up were any indication, she'd accomplished that last one with flying colors.

Numerous times on the way into town, he'd glanced across the front seat of the truck and opened his mouth as if to say something, then swallowed and stared straight ahead.

Thankfully Ruby had jabbered from the back seat the whole way into town.

And it wasn't helping matters that Luc wore a short-sleeved plaid button-down, jeans and square-toed boots. The man cleaned up well. He'd shaved, the faint smell of lotion mingling with his typical scent in the cab of the truck.

They parked in the overflow parking— pretty much a field of run-down grass, weeds and dirt. Carnival-like sounds and the sugary-sweet aroma of cotton candy drifted across the summer night air as they got out.

"Can I have a treat?" Ruby's pleading

caused her and Luc to share an amused look. They hadn't even taken a step yet.

"Maybe in a little bit," Cate answered.

"I agree with your mother," Luc added before Ruby could beg him for a different outcome. "The ground is kind of muddy from the rain. Probably should have dropped you girls off."

The downpour overnight had been hard and fast, drumming against the cabin roof. Luc snatched up Ruby, holding her on his left side. "I'll carry you over the bad part." She'd worn her pink sandals with a white sundress. One Cate would surely have to bleach by the end of the night. But when Ruby had requested to wear a dress so she "looked like Mom," Cate hadn't been able to refuse.

"Here." Luc held out his right hand to her.

What was she supposed to do with it?

"The ground's uneven. I'll just steady you until we're out of the lot."

She eyed her strappy wedges that peeked

out below the midcalf hem of her sundress. "Guess I should have worn more logical shoes."

Though Cate had been feeling anything but. She and Ruby had enjoyed getting ready. Cate would like to think it was just because they were getting a night out. But one greedy glance at Luc told her otherwise.

"I'm not complaining." Luc's quip held a grin and more. A message she wasn't sure she should read.

She took his hand. What was a girl supposed to do? Raising a fuss about it would only make her feelings more known.

Once they made it across the overflow lot, Luc released her hand and plunked Ruby on the ground. The absence of his touch wove through her, a foreshadowing of the week to come.

Ruby spotted the red-and-blue bounce house and took off in a run. They followed.

She got in line, and within a few minutes she was romping with her new friends from church—two little girls whom she'd hit it off with in Sunday school.

Cate spotted Emma across the churchyard and waved. She walked toward them, holding the hands of two little boys, one a few inches taller than the other.

"Hey, guys. These two are my dates for the evening." Emma introduced them just as a cry came from inside the bounce house.

Didn't sound like Ruby, but Cate should probably check.

"I'll make sure Ruby's okay." Luc read her mind and strode across the grass. She stole a glance or three at his retreating back. Was there anything more attractive than Luc being a father? Cate didn't think so.

She snapped her attention back to Emma before she got caught. "What are your friends up to tonight? You never said."

"Date night. They were in desperate need and I had nothing going on, so I offered to bring the boys down here."

"You're the best. I could have used a friend like you when I first had Ruby."

"Well, you've got me now. Anytime you need anything, even in Denver, let me know."

"Thanks." That meant a lot. It was so Emma to do for everyone else and act like nothing made her happier. "Did you at least relax a little today?"

"Yep." Emma's peaches-and-cream complexion shone with contentment. "I went out to the hot springs for a bit and read a book. It was a good day." Her eyebrows wiggled. "By the way, you look beautiful tonight."

Heat singed Cate's cheeks. "I'm over-dressed, aren't I?" Especially considering Emma wore black shorts and a T-shirt that said *I was country before country as cool* in yellow letters over gray. Coupled with charcoal Converse, she had irresistible down to a science. Funny that Emma never talked about dating. Never mentioned any guys she might be interested in. Cate wanted to ask, but the opportunity to probe had never presented itself.

"Not in the least. Your dress is perfect for a night out. And I'm sure my idiot brother hasn't said a thing about how gorgeous you look." Emma punctuated the sentence with a huff.

Cate laughed, neither confirming nor denying. Though they had been with Ruby. That might have been awkward if he had said something. Or maybe he hadn't noticed her at all and she'd only imagined his interest earlier.

Luc came back to them just as the boys lost their patience and began clambering to go in the bouncy house.

"Ruby's fine. It was one of the other kids."

"You guys should leave Ruby with me for a bit," Emma offered. "Go walk around town. I'll be here anyway. No reason we all have to stay."

She and Luc most definitely did not need alone time. And Cate loved being near Ruby.

Always had. Being with Luc minus the buffer of Ruby *did* sound like a date.

"I guess we could." Luc's questioning gaze landed on Cate. "What do you think?"

"Don't ask, Lucas Wilder," Emma called over her shoulder as the boys dragged her toward the wildly moving bounce house filled with screeching children. "If she's smart, she'll come up with any reason to avoid you." She beamed with little-sister victory and sass.

When Ruby slid out to let a new group in, Emma bent to speak with her. Ruby's head bobbed, and Emma waved at them. Dismissed. Just like that.

A rush of uncomfortableness and a hint of anticipation danced across Cate's nerves at the idea of time with Luc. Just the two of them.

"Okay, then. Guess we're not needed here." A grin that would cause any woman in a one-hundred-mile radius to sigh surfaced on Luc's handsome mug. "Let's walk. You okay in those shoes?"

"You okay in those boots?"

He laughed.

The sound of kids giggling and people talking faded to a quiet hum as they hit the Main Street sidewalk. A few of the stores had sale items out on tables or hanging on racks. Others had their doors propped open with welcome signs placed prominently in the windows.

Cate perused a table of clearance kids' clothing. Not a huge selection, but one pair of snow boots that might fit Ruby over the winter. Still a little out of her price range. She could probably get them for less if she shopped online or in a mom swap group. As they left that storefront, a group of teens strolled by, not noticing them and almost plowing into her. Luc grabbed her hand, nudging her behind him. Protective man.

But once the kids passed and they walked again, he didn't let go.

She wasn't sure whether to be flattered or concerned or try to run. All three sounded like good options. Luc's fingers loosened. Cate held her breath. But then he simply switched from cupping her hand to threading his fingers through hers. Her stomach dipped and rolled. Being with Luc like this felt like coming home after far too long. But those thoughts shouldn't be on her radar. She was supposed to be thinking about her daughter and not herself. The opposite of what her parents had done.

Still, she could relax about a little handholding, couldn't she? Even if it was making her mind flood with memories of when she and Luc had been inseparable. Back then he'd always held her hand…if he was driving. Or walking. Breathing.

Oh, man. This was exactly why she should be running from him right now.

At the local fudge shop they stopped for a free sample. The taste of salted caramel lingered on Cate's tongue as they exited the small store.

"I was thinking—" Luc nudged her shoulder with his "—since we don't have Ruby with us—and she's perfectly well taken care of by Emma—that maybe we can just be us. One night off from parenting. From only focusing on Ruby. We can allow ourselves that, can't we?"

Ever since Ruby was born, Cate hadn't let her guard down. Not once. Through all of the medical appointments. The diagnosis. The sleepless nights and long days of work. Her mind churned with the mistakes she wanted to avoid making and this precious time with Luc she so badly wanted. Maybe even needed.

"I'll take that as a yes." Luc's hand squeezed hers, and Cate opened her mouth to protest, but not even a squeak came out. So much for standing strong. She was already entangled with him, and they hadn't even been alone for ten minutes. What did that say about her? Maybe it said she was human. And a girl who'd once loved a boy with all of her broken pieces. For a few moments she wanted to not overthink.

Besides, what would be the harm in one night off?

Chapter Thirteen

Luc had set a lot of boundaries for himself regarding Cate, and tonight he'd leaped
right over them without a backward glance.
Stupid? Probably. But Cate's hand was currently linked with his, and after he'd touched
her, his logical senses had signed off for the
night.

"So I've been meaning to ask you something." Cate peeked at him through a layer
of her warm brown hair. It was down tonight
with a slight curl.

Yes, you and Ruby can stay at the ranch.
You fit so well. I was thinking the same thing.

He barely tamped down a snort at his foolish thoughts. "What's on your mind?"

"I love your ranch slogan. 'Get out in the wild.' It's perfect."

"Thanks. That's not a question."

"Who designed your shirts and made your logo?"

Luc racked his brain. "I think some kid that worked for us a long time ago. Not sure I remember. Why?" Her teeth pressed into her upper lip. Buying time? Why did she hesitate to answer? "Whatever it is, just say it."

"Okay." Cate paused, facing him. "You could use a new logo." Curving lips softened the statement. "It's too bad you don't know anyone who could help you out with that. Pro bono."

"That is too bad."

She whacked him on the arm, and he began walking again, keeping her with him. Not planning to let go of her anytime soon. And if he only had tonight, he'd like to add that kiss he'd been preoccupied with to their list of things to do.

"So will you let me do it? I have an idea already."

"Let you? Of course. If you really want to. Are you sure you have time?"

"I'll make time. Being at the ranch has been good for me. For Ruby. I know I wasn't keen on the idea, but it's been nice. It would be fun to do something for the ranch in return."

If only his body didn't flood with hope. She'd said the ranch, not him. He could read between the lines all he wanted, but that didn't change the truth.

They'd reached the end of most of the stores on their side of Main Street, so they crossed over at the stop sign. No traffic light yet, though there'd been talk about it in the local paper.

"Now that you've had more time here, what do you think of Westbend?"

"I like it. It's quaint. Welcoming. Even

church has been good. I expected some judgment in a small town like this." She tipped her head in his direction. "For our situation. But so far I've only found kindness."

"If anyone treated you badly, I'd want to know."

Her lips pressed together as if resisting a smile. "What would you do? Beat them up?"

"No." A chuckle shook his chest. "But I'd say something. We both made decisions back then. And we've both changed."

It was true. They had. Luc believed differently now, just like Cate did. Neither of them would have the kind of physical relationship in the present that they'd had in the past. Not until his finger had a wedding band on it. Because now he understood intimacy meant so much more than what he'd believed at nineteen.

Just like his parents had tried to teach him when he hadn't been listening.

"By the way, my parents are planning a trip. They want to meet Ruby and you.

Think you'd be willing to come out to the ranch for dinner when they're here?" Luc had been talking to them quite a bit. Filling them in. His mom had even commented that his tone regarding Cate had changed recently. Funny that she could tell from so many miles away.

A shaky breath came from Cate. "Wow. I guess. I'd be so nervous. Don't they hate me?"

He squeezed her hand, the answering pressure from her doing things to his insides he didn't want to acknowledge. "You don't need to be. It took them a bit to wrap their minds around having a granddaughter. But I've been sending them pictures of Ruby and they're already her biggest fans. They've come around quickly even though it was unexpected."

"Well, you forgave me." Cate squared her shoulders. "Guess I'll just have to pray they can, too."

Luc liked seeing Cate reach for faith. It

was an attractive quality. Not that he needed to add any more to the many she already had.

"How are things with Mackenzie? Any better?"

Cate had confided in him that she wasn't sure Mackenzie could forgive her for what she'd done. But he'd told her that was just Kenzie's way—protective like a bear with her cubs. And that she'd come around with time. She'd better, or he'd get after her about it. Luc was trying to be patient. To give the two of them the space to work things out without his interference.

"A little bit, actually. The interesting thing about her is that I think I could trust her with Ruby's life, even if she's not sure about me."

And…that was his sister to a T. "Sounds right."

"I want her to like me, but at the same time… I don't deserve it."

"None of us deserves anything, really. We're all messes redeemed by God's grace.

But I get what you're saying. You want her to believe your heart is good. You want her to see you for who you are, not what you've done."

"Yes!" She brightened. "That's exactly what I want. How I feel."

"Back when…" He paused. Swallowed. Was he really broaching this subject? Cate always skirted around their history, but Luc needed to talk about it. Might as well be now. "That's what I wanted from you, too, back when you asked if I was seeing someone else. I needed you to believe me. To know that I would never do something like that. And I couldn't imagine how you thought otherwise. That's why I lost it and left. You not trusting me just about killed me."

Her pretty face contorted with pain, which hadn't been his intent. He just wanted her to understand why it mattered so much.

Luc continued. "When I was a sophomore in high school, I was accused of vandalism with some friends. I didn't do it, but even my parents didn't believe me. I was so frustrated by their lack of trust. Hated that feeling. And when it repeated with you..." Agitation rose up, choking him. "So much worse." Understatement of his life. Because he'd loved her with every single cell in his body.

Just like he did now.

The thought might have surprised him, but Luc instantly felt its truth. Cate had swept back into his life, conjuring a snowstorm of emotions. Anger at first. Then frustration, confusion, hurt. And now...love. Though if he had to guess, that one had been hiding in plain sight all along.

She didn't trust him as far as she could throw him, and yet he loved her. He couldn't help it. It was like he'd been born a match for her, and he refused any other options.

But what could he do about it?

There was still too much unresolved between them. Loving her wouldn't fix everything. Plus, Cate wasn't ready to hear the words tumbling around in his head. If he said them right now, she might run. And Luc was nowhere near ready to lose her all over again.

"I hate that I did that to you." Cate should have known better, but at the time, she'd been young and immature. She'd let herself be swayed against believing Luc when that was exactly what she'd wanted to do. She'd been afraid to be wrong. To be one of those girls who accepted a smooth answer only to find out later that she'd been a fool.

"When Roark first told me that he'd spotted you with some other woman, I didn't believe him. My first thought was to trust you. But he had so many details, I couldn't imagine that he'd made it all up. And then I panicked, thinking I'd missed something. That you weren't who I thought you were."

Luc stopped so fast that his hand, still entwined with hers, brought her to a screeching halt. "Roark? What does he have to do with anything?"

"He's the one who told me."

His eyelids momentarily slammed shut. "Well, no wonder. Now it all makes sense."

"What do you mean?"

"Roark had a thing for you. I knew it the first time you introduced us."

"There's no way." Her head shook vehemently.

A twitch started in Luc's jaw. "Where did he say he saw me?"

"Park Meadows Mall. Holding hands with another woman. Kissing her." The confession hissed from her lips, causing a stabbing pain all over again.

A groan/laugh combination escaped from Luc and she barely resisted a slap to his face. How could he find humor in something like that? When Roark had told her, she'd crumbled into a thousand pieces.

Luc bent so that his eyes were inches from hers. Direct. Mesmerizing. "When in your life have you ever known me to go shopping? I've never even been to that mall. He made it up, Cate. Spun a story to get to you."

"But I don't think he would—" No. Couldn't be. But at the same time, Luc was right. That wasn't something he would do—someplace he would be. Even then, the story hadn't quite fit. Hadn't made sense.

"Did he ask you out after we broke up?"

Her head bobbed. "Yes. Wouldn't take no for an answer until I found out I was pregnant with Ruby. After I told him that, he left me alone." Her hands were both entangled with his now, fingers squeezing life and apology. What had she done? What had they done? "Luc, I'm so sorry. I didn't know. I'd grown up with Roark. Our families were friends. I didn't have any reason not to believe him."

"But you had a reason not to believe me?"

Ouch. "I wanted to, but I was scared. And the more questions I asked, the more you shut down."

This was what she'd wanted to know back

when they were twenty. And finding out now, after all of this time...after she'd kept Ruby from him... Cate didn't know whether to cry or scream.

"I was too immature to answer you then." Luc cradled her face, and she pressed her cheek into his warm palm, needing the comfort he offered. "All I could think about was you not trusting me." His sigh wrenched between them. "I didn't handle any of it well. I should have listened and explained. I should have fought for you, not with you. I'm sorry, Cate."

"Me, too." So much. Why hadn't she gone with her instinct back then? Said more— something, *anything* but heightened accusations. Why hadn't he? They'd been young, but that wasn't a worthy excuse for how they'd treated each other.

They couldn't change the decisions they'd made, but they could redirect the future. She wanted them to disassemble the jail cell they'd unknowingly built together. That had trapped them under assumptions.

"Lucas, do you think it's possible for us to let go of what happened?"

Why couldn't she breathe? Had her respiratory system gone on vacation? Her vision blurred, Luc's smooth jaw waning in and out of focus. Everything in her waited for his response, time standing still. She could survive without him. She'd done it before. But she didn't want to do it again. Even if it was just friendship—and Ruby—keeping them connected, she needed him.

His hands moved farther into her hair, kneading her neck while her muscles waved a white flag of surrender.

His Adam's apple bobbed as he gave a definite nod, then gathered her against his chest as if she was made of sugar and spice and everything nice. If holding was a school subject, Luc would earn an A+ every semester. Wrapping her up tight had always been his go-to—though she wasn't sure he even realized it. He'd done the same last week just before she'd confessed her fears to him.

He had the best grip—tight enough to feel wanted. Safe. Not so constraining that she couldn't budge.

Unwinding started at the top of her head, swirling down her body until even her toes felt the change.

When he loosened, she moved back, but barely. Somewhere in the exit from his delicious embrace, her hands had slid up his arms. Currently they were wrapped around his biceps like it was her job to check their circumference.

Luc? Professional holder. For her only, of course.

Cate? Measuring each of Luc's chiseled muscles one at a time.

His gaze dropped to her lips and held, enough tension and anticipation to supply the city of Westbend with all the electrical current needed for a month.

Would he kiss her? Did she want him

to? The answers to those questions came quickly: he'd better, and *yes*.

A rush of impatience gripped her like Ruby in a candy store, wanting it all and despising the line. Cate had told herself numerous times Luc wasn't hers to have. To take home for keeps. She'd believed she was doomed to repeat her parents' mistakes. That she and Luc revisiting their relationship would only end in brokenness.

What if she'd been wrong all along?

Five seconds earlier Luc would have been able to repeat his and Cate's conversation, but the last few moments had completely erased that possibility.

When had they gone from talking to tangled up in the middle of a sidewalk? Like they could erase the hurt between them with each other's touch?

Luc was definitely willing to give that theory the old college try. He wanted nothing more than to kiss Cate, but all kinds of warning sirens blared. Would he ruin everything they'd just bandaged if he did?

Did she want the same?

She'd had ample opportunity to scoot back after he'd hugged her in answer to her question. Could they move on? Start over? Leave it all behind?

Check the yes box for him.

Luc memorized her mouth like a starved man, though the reminder wasn't necessary. The details had been singed into his brain years ago. When their eyes met, hers were brimming with… That couldn't be love, could it? No. But maybe something close. Like. Interest.

Invitation.

Hopefully, he hadn't read that last one wrong, because Luc was done waiting for a hand-addressed envelope to show up in his mailbox. He brushed her lips with his, planning to wait for her response—to see if she'd pull away. But his patience flew out the window the moment their mouths met.

Her hands slid behind his neck, and the street noises muffled as the sound of his pulse roared in his ears. It had been so long since he'd kissed Cate. He held on, praying for healing for all of the sorrow they'd caused each other. Wanting their connection to make it all disappear.

Maybe she needed the same comfort he did. But this was far more than a Band-Aid for their mistakes. This was what he wanted for the future.

Luc eased slightly from her magnetic pull.

In a matter of minutes they'd gone from digging up the past, to burying it, to creating something fresh. Luc liked that last one the best. Because this Cate was a mix of old and new woven together. The mother of his child. His first love and his second, and he never wanted to stop kissing her.

So he didn't.

He swooped in for one more taste. What if he'd been wrong earlier? What if there was a chance she could love him again? He wasn't lazy. He would work himself to the bone to make that happen. If only she could trust him.

He was definitely in love with Cate all over again. Not in a childish way this time, but in a way he'd never experienced before. He wanted a life with Ruby and Cate. Wanted to fight for that. There was no going back. With Ruby to consider, they'd have to be fully committed. And he was. But was she? Knowing her, she'd need time to process. If he pushed right now, she'd scatter like raindrops on a windshield. One swipe and gone forever.

Voices sounded, exiting from the coffee shop two doors down, cutting off their *just one more kiss* that had heated faster than metal reflecting the Colorado sun.

Cate stepped back, amusement evident. Her jaw tipped up, a sassy little move that only tempted him to head in that direction next. She was a mix of shy and sweet, embarrassed and yet refusing to give in to that last emotion. "Maybe in the middle of town isn't the best place for our second first kiss."

Second first. He liked the sound of that. A grin spread so wide it stretched the skin tight over his cheekbones. "You're probably right. Have I told you how beautiful you look tonight?"

She answered with a slowly shaking head, doubt shadowing the playfulness sparkling in her eyes. "I think I'm too dressed up for such a casual night."

"I think you're perfect." He'd wanted to tell her in the truck earlier that she looked gorgeous, but he'd been hesitant to say something like that in front of Ruby. "There aren't enough words in the dictionary to do you justice, Catherine Malory." Luc didn't allow her the time to protest. Instead, he tucked her close and held on as they began walking.

If only he could be confident the future held more of the same.

Chapter Fourteen

⁓

What had she done? What had they done? This was why Cate didn't take time off from focusing on Ruby. Because the lapse left her awake in the middle of the night, sheets twisted from her tossing and turning, heart beating out a rhythm of mingled fear and hope while she wrestled with the knowledge that if Luc walked through the door right now, she'd kiss him all over again.

Last night after their walk through town, she and Luc had gone back to the church to spend the rest of the evening with Ruby. Cate had relished their time together—all three of them. The night had been something close to perfect, at least in her mind. On their way home Ruby had conked out in the truck. Luc had carried her inside and tucked her in. Then he'd pulled Cate out to the front step to say good-night. He'd been so…careful with her. Like she was a precious gift he wanted to wait to unwrap. He'd held her for a long minute, kissed her cheek, and then he'd been gone before she could decipher the many emotions flitting across his features.

The man was more tempting than tiramisu crafted from the aged hands of an Italian grandmother.

Cate attempted to retuck the fitted sheet that had recently slipped free from the corner of the mattress. When her efforts didn't pan out, she tore out of the bed and gave it a strong tug, taking a moment to realign everything her worries had tangled during the night.

What kind of monster could sleep in disheveled sheets?

Prim gave a meow from her spot in the corner that sounded strangely like a sigh. Cate's antics had woken the princess.

After opening the bedroom window to let in cooler air, Cate plopped back into bed and glanced at the time. Five in the morning. So not exactly the middle of the night, but her exhausted body told her she hadn't gained much in the way of sleep in the hours before.

She ran her hand over Prim's back as the cat slunk along the edge of the mattress. Prim paused to accept the comfort she offered. A bit like Cate had done last night when she'd broken all of her self-imposed rules and leaned into Lucas.

"I wasn't that bad."

Prim meowed.

"Okay, so I like him." She scooped Prim onto her lap, easing back against the headboard in a sitting position. Why pretend sleep would come at all?

Cate would be lying to herself if she didn't acknowledge that Luc had always held on to a portion of her heart. They'd never been over and done. And not just because Ruby linked them together as parents. But because he was Lucas. And she needed him far more than she wanted to admit.

So much for all of the plans and stopgaps she'd set in place to keep this exact thing from happening.

Cate must have squeezed Prim a bit too hard—frustration surfacing in her grip— because the cat tossed her head with snotty annoyance and escaped from Cate's lap to curl up on the other side of the bed. Her narrowed eyes seemed to say, *Pull yourself together, girl.*

"I'm just trying to figure things out."

Prim's eyelids grew heavy, head resting on her paws.

"And you're a rotten sounding board as usual. Where's your good advice, huh?"

The cat's spine lifted and fell with each

steady breath. Once again, Cate was talking to her pet and expecting answers.

She groaned. "I'm totally going to become an old cat lady who carries on conversations with her tabby. I'm already halfway there. A few more years and some gray hairs—goal met."

Cate punched the pillow into submission and slumped down on her side, staring at the alarm clock on the nightstand.

Obviously she had feelings for Luc. She didn't need anyone to listen to her—Prim included—to know that. They'd worked out the past, and she felt peace. Cate could finally allow herself to believe what she'd wanted to all along. That Luc would never have done what Roark accused him of. What a jerk Roark had been to throw fake stones like that.

And she'd been distrusting enough to listen.

Shame on her.

But what now? Luc hadn't said anything

about the future. Could they actually attempt a relationship again? Did he want to? They couldn't be wishy-washy. They didn't have that liberty...not as Ruby's parents. Cate needed to know what he was thinking. For her sake and for Ruby's. Because she *would not* let a relationship between them—or even the possibility of it—hurt their daughter.

By the time six thirty rolled around, Cate had showered and dressed in a soft pink shirt and flowered pencil skirt she could wear to church. She applied makeup and did her hair, then paced back and forth in her bedroom, praying. Asking for wisdom not to make the same mistakes she had last time. Even praying that she would remain open. Cate struggled with that after watching her parents make so many blunders. It was painfully hard for her to believe there were people in the world who could love each other unconditionally.

But what if she and Luc were the exception

to the rule? She had to talk to him. Should she call? Text? No. It had to be in person.

Cate checked on Ruby—still asleep.

The girl never slept in, but today she showed no signs of waking. Each second Cate waited to get answers from Luc aggravated like someone smacking gum inches from her ear.

She retreated to the living room. The house where Luc was crashing with his sisters was just a few steps down the hill. Within sight. Cate could run over, see if he was home and be back before Ruby woke.

She slid on black sandals and flew down the hill, knocking lightly on the front door.

Please let Luc answer. Please let Luc answer.

The wooden interior door unlocked, Mackenzie visible as it swung wide. She pushed the screen door open. "Cate?"

Really, God? You couldn't even give me Emma?

For a second Cate cowered. But then she

pressed her shoulders back. She was on a mission, and even Luc's intimidating sister couldn't stop her.

But exactly how long had Mackenzie been awake? Her hair flowed in waves, a yellow T-shirt and shorts spitting two of the longest, tannest legs into the universe.

"Do you just roll out of bed looking like that?" *Whoops.* Based on Mackenzie's laughter, she'd actually just said that out loud.

The skin around Mackenzie's unique gray-blue eyes crinkled with enough kindness to give Cate courage. "Everything okay?"

"Yes." *No.* "Is Luc here? I need to speak with him."

"He left a bit ago. He's an early riser, but I don't know where he's off to on a Sunday." Mackenzie had a toothbrush in her hand, and she pointed toward the lodge with it. "Might try his office."

"Thanks." Cate took a step back, then glanced at her cabin. She couldn't leave

Ruby alone. She'd just have to calm down like a big girl and wait it out.

Mackenzie studied her. "Do you need me to stay with Ruby while you go talk to him?"

What? Seriously? Mackenzie might not be waving a big white truce flag, but she wasn't snarling, either. Maybe the woman was coming around.

Was accepting her help the right thing to do? Cate was desperate to calm the questions swirling inside her. "Yes. Please. She's asleep right now."

"Just like her aunt Emma." A flash of white teeth and Mackenzie disappeared inside, leaving the door open. And then she was back, toothbrush discarded, flip-flops on. The door clicked shut behind her.

Cate didn't move. Her shoes had suddenly become very attached to the ground directly beneath her.

"Go ahead." Mackenzie nodded toward the lodge. "I may not be Emma but I can handle hanging out with my niece, whether she's asleep or awake. We'll be fine."

Little did Mackenzie know that wasn't the issue tying Cate into knots.

No more overthinking. Cate would lose her resolve if she waited any longer. After a thank-you to Mackenzie, she hurried to the lodge.

When she knocked on Luc's office door, he didn't answer. "Lucas?" She twisted the knob and peeked inside. The lights weren't on.

Cate paused at the threshold. He could be over in the barn. Or somewhere else in the lodge. But if she went looking for him, she'd likely miss him.

She'd wait in his office for a few minutes and see if he showed.

Cate flipped on the light switch and then sat on the futon that faced Luc's desk. After a few minutes she jumped up, nerves making her limbs twitchy. She crossed to the far window. It showcased the sprawling ranch like a framed photograph, morning light dancing across dew-dampened grass.

Unable to stay still for more than three seconds and feeling a little like Ruby, Cate turned and strode by the desk, her hand bumping a stack of papers perched on the corner. They jostled, and she began straightening them. She couldn't handle it when the edges didn't match up in perfect symmetry.

The words *parental responsibilities* popped out from the top corner of one located at the bottom, and her body morphed into a glacier. That fancy phrase translated into custody.

"I should ignore it." She stared at the wall above the futon, begging one of the family photos there to capture her attention. "It's probably just a guest's paperwork. Nothing to do with me or Ruby."

Just like Prim, the walls didn't answer her.

Abandoning her OCD task, Cate scooted back to the futon and dropped down. But suspicion slithered in through the cracks of her broken pieces. The papers called out, mocking her.

What if she looked? Proved her concerns wrong? She could do that, couldn't she?

Cate lunged for the desk, quickly shuffling to the bottom of the stack. The paper-clipped sheets revealed more than her trembling limbs could handle. Information about how to file for custody lined the pages, a hand-written note in blue ink scrawled across the top of the first page: *Lucas, call with any questions or to set up a meeting.* The phone number beneath it blurred through her watery vision.

The room tilted, and she closed her eyes against the sensation of free-falling.

No way. She didn't believe it. Not after what they'd talked about. How close they'd gotten. After last night.

Luc might not have said how he felt, but hadn't she read his feelings loud and clear?

Had it all been a lie to get her to let down her guard? So that he had time to pursue custody? Her teeth chattered, the shaking transferring through her whole body.

And to think, she'd believed him. Trusted him with not only herself, but Ruby, too. She should have known better. Some people got second chances.

She just wasn't one of them.

Cate's looking for you. I sent her to your office.

Luc palmed his phone, the time stamp on Mackenzie's text from fifteen minutes before.

Was it a good or bad sign that Cate was up early, wanting to see him? *Please, please let it be the first.*

This morning he'd woken before the sun, finally given up on sleep and headed out for a ride. Some time to process and talk to God about the restless fears holding his head under water. He'd left his phone in his room.

Now he slid it into his back pocket and beelined for the lodge.

For weeks Luc had been capsized by the idea that Cate would never truly trust him. And even after discovering Roark's part in what had happened, he hadn't told her he loved her. He'd been afraid that she wasn't ready to hear it. That their past could still so easily repeat itself. But after venting it all out to God, he felt renewed. Luc worshipped the King of mercy and miracles and second chances. He could trust in that. In Him.

He'd been a wuss not telling Cate how he felt last night, and he refused to hide behind lame excuses any longer.

Luc still had part of today with Cate and Ruby here, and he would rectify his mistake. He needed to tell Cate he was so far gone, he couldn't stop loving her if he tried. He loved everything about her. The way she clung to control and the sweet victory when she released things from her iron grip, handing them over ever so slowly to God's keeping. Her fierce protectiveness of Ruby. And then there was the way she looked at him when she let him in…like there wasn't anywhere else in the world she'd rather be. Like he was her safety net. He craved all of her. Even the battle scars from her childhood that had shaped her into being strong and vulnerable at the same time. He was unwilling to live without her and Ruby in his life. Luc wanted the three of them to be a family, not spread out over two cities and thousands of acres of land.

And if he had to wait for her feelings to catch up with his, that was exactly what he would do.

Luc flew up the lodge steps and through the lobby. His office door was open. Inside, Cate stood next to his desk. She wore a straight flowered skirt, a light pink shirt and sandals. Her hair was down with a slight curl. The most beautiful woman in the world had not only crashed back into his life, but she'd also given him the best daughter he could ever ask for.

He blinked back emotion as he crossed

the space. "Hey." His voice came out low, somehow managing to crack one syllable into two. He captured her in an embrace that scooped her off the ground. It felt *so good* to hold her. To think that she could actually be his again and he could be hers.

After he and Cate split, Luc had thought he might never feel about anyone the way he had about her. Turned out, he'd been right. She was *it* for him.

Here he was, right back in love with her all over again.

"Nine hours is way too long to be separated from you. We're going to have to figure out another system." One with a wedding ring, if he had anything to say about it. "Woman, you are not conducive to good sleep." He pressed a kiss against her neck, considering the flesh that rose in goose bumps as a good sign.

But then again, maybe he was jumping the gun... Cate's arms hadn't reciprocated.

She didn't shove away, but she hung against him like a limp, lifeless baby doll of Ruby's.

Concern spread through him, and he eased her feet back to the floor.

"What's going on? You okay?"

"No." She hugged herself, hands scrubbing along her upper arms.

Maybe he'd confused her last night by not stating clearly how he felt. "Listen, Cate, about—"

"What are these?"

She lifted a stack of papers from the desk. Her eyes were cold. None of the warmth and openness from the evening before remained. Like a switch had been turned.

Invisible fists gripped his windpipe, crushing any chance for air. *No, no, no.* Luc hadn't been back in the office since Friday when Gage had dropped the papers off...when he'd been wanting to get Cate out of here so that she wouldn't see them. He'd spent Saturday with Cate and Ruby and hadn't given the custody info a second thought.

Why hadn't he come in just to throw them away? Or torch them? Dread edged along his spine. Luc needed to convince Cate that what she held wasn't the truth. He edged to block her path to the door, buying himself time.

"They're not what you think."

"Really? They're not filled with information about you filing for custody of Ruby?" She sounded hollow. Shattered.

Of course they were. Stupid, stupid move on his part. He'd like to blame Gage, but Luc was the one who'd given him the go-ahead in the first place.

"Gage offered to help me way back in the beginning. When you showed up with Ruby and I didn't know what to do. I was concerned that you could just take her and disappear, so I told him to look into it."

Luc wasn't going to make the mistake of not completely discussing everything like the last time. He and Cate needed full disclosure. He kept his voice easy. Nonconfrontational. He had nothing to hide. He should have just told Cate about the papers after Gage had dropped them off on Friday. Explained everything to her then. If he had, maybe he wouldn't be in this situation right now, panicking that this was the final nail in the coffin of their momentary second chance. But he hadn't said anything because he'd worried that she would react exactly like she was now.

"He brought them in Friday afternoon. I told him I wasn't interested anymore. That you and I were going to work things out. He left them here, and I planned to throw them away. I just haven't been in the office since then. I've been with you and Ruby, and I didn't think about those papers once over the weekend. That has to tell you something."

Luc prayed that Cate would really hear him, but she looked vacant. A listless shell that didn't register his defense.

Desperation took root. He grabbed her arms. "I love you, Cate. I wasn't going to follow through on the custody stuff. I know how much that scares you. Are you hearing me?"

No answer.

Luc didn't know what to do. Kiss her? She'd slap him. Trap her here and hold her captive until she accepted his explanation?

"Remember everything we talked about last night? You didn't believe me when we were twenty and we lost four years. Don't do that this time. You can trust me. I promise." He inched closer, celebrating a surge of victory when she didn't immediately shrink away. The hold he had around her wrists softened, thumbs tracing over her jumpy pulse. "I need you to believe me, Cate. Please."

"I can't." She retreated, stark trauma written in the bruised half-moons under her eyes.

"Why not? You said you should have last time. Why can't you now?"

"Last time I didn't have proof." The papers shook in her hand. "This time I do."

She shoved them against his chest, jutted around him and ran from his office as the mess fluttered to the floor.

His rib cage exploded with pressure, the repaired organ in his chest giving signs of surrender.

All of this time he'd questioned if Cate would choose to trust him moving forward. Now he had his answer.

Chapter Fifteen

The boom of the twelve-gauge shotgun echoed from the surrounding hills as Luc caught the next clay target in his sight and pulled the trigger.

"It's about to storm. Wasn't sure if you'd noticed," Mackenzie called out from behind him, her sarcasm as thick as the charcoal clouds rolling in. Luc took one more shot before switching the trap thrower to the off position.

He perched his gun on the wooden holding rack and faced her, sliding his ear protection to the back of his neck.

"I noticed." The sky touching the pine-covered hills was dark and vicious, but so far no rain had fallen. No thunder or lightning yet.

Luc had run the afternoon skeet session for the guests. Once they finished up, he'd sent them back to the ranch, leaving the cleanup for himself. But he hadn't been able to resist a few rounds before packing everything into the back of the truck.

"You just out here sulking?"

"Shooting. Not sulking." Actually, Luc thought he'd done a pretty good job of keeping it together since Cate and Ruby had left on Sunday. He hadn't yelled at anyone. Family or staff. Hadn't lost his temper. No tantrums or outbursts. Mostly, he'd just been quietly stewing over things. Though he'd yet to come up with any answers.

The worst part had been the conversation with Cate after she'd packed up.

"Here." She'd handed him a piece of paper. "This is a possible list of times for you to have Ruby. Built around your time off. Look it over and see what you think or if you want to change anything. We can adjust when you move to the fall schedule."

No tears. No *maybe I made a mistake in not believing you.* Cate had switched off her emotions like a garden hose. One twist—done.

Luc didn't have the same ability. It had taken everything in him not to say something more to her. But what? Her response to his explanation on Sunday morning had been to storm out of his office. Had she even heard him say he loved her? She'd certainly never acknowledged his declaration.

Mackenzie braced hands on her hips, stance wide. "Have you heard from Cate?"

Only in email. She'd sent him new logo options for the ranch, of all things. Their arrival in his inbox had sent his pulse skyrocketing, making him wonder if she'd changed her mind. Until he'd realized it was all business. *Choose one. Let me know. I can tweak it.*

That had been it.

The funny part was, the first logo was perfect. She'd captured the feel of the ranch, yet she didn't want to be anywhere near it or him.

Go figure.

He retrieved a box of shells that had tumbled to the grass and tossed it into the plastic bin on the tailgate. "Why do you care? You never liked her anyway."

"Not true. I took my time getting to know her. Didn't trust her at first."

"And now?"

"She's grown on me. Probably stemming from the fact that she and Ruby make you happy. Believe it or not, I want that for you."

Luc let out a half grunt, half laugh. "Well, you're going to have to deal with a brother who's not all sunshine and rainbows, because Cate wants nothing to do with me."

"That's not what I gathered when she showed up on our step Sunday morning."

Before everything had imploded into a

fiery mess. "Then your detective skills are wrong." Last time Luc had fought with Cate, he'd been young and angry. Now, in the course of four years, he felt old and worn. Sadness hung around him. Despair permeated his body. They'd done this one too many times. She'd chosen not to trust him one too many times. How could he overlook that?

"You do realize that I know you're upset, right? It's not like I can just turn off the twin connection when you're being annoying."

A sigh leaked from his chest. "Just give me some space. I'll get over her again. It just takes time." Unfortunately, he knew from experience.

"Why?"

"Why what?"

"Why get over her? You two are connected by Ruby. But I think there's more than that to what you have."

He'd thought so, too. Luc had been positive he and Cate had earned their second chance over the past month.

"The two of you will always be in each other's lives because of your daughter. So what do you want that relationship to look like?"

Mackenzie's question strangled him. Like a family. That was what he wanted. But he couldn't just ignore the fact that Cate had once again tossed him into the gutter. How could a relationship be built on that?

"The way I see it, you can spend the rest of your life fighting with her, or for her."

Luc's jaw unhinged. "Are you seriously giving me dating advice? Love advice? You, who hasn't—"

"Lucas Wilder, we're not talking about me. We're talking about you. Don't change the subject." Mackenzie's *don't mess with me* expression told Luc he didn't stand a chance of winning this argument.

"Fine. You're right. I'm wrong. Are we done now?"

Her exaggerated groan cut into the air as Luc spotted Gage heading in their direction.

Great. Another person coming to poke and prod?

"I give up." Mackenzie whirled toward the lodge and shoved a finger at Gage as he neared them. "You handle him. I tried." And then she was off, her boots raising up dust, agitation and disapproval evident in every step.

"You come to yell at me, too?"

"Me? Never." Gage retrieved a twenty-gauge shotgun from the wooden holder and loaded it.

This was Luc's kind of conversation. He reloaded, and when both of them were ready, he flipped the trap thrower switch to On. Blasts reigned for the next few minutes as the two of them took turns demolishing orange flying targets.

Almost gave his grief a place to hold on to.

When a raindrop hit him on the forearm,

Luc turned off the machine. He and Gage began packing up.

"Emma told me something went south between you and Cate, though she didn't give me details. I'm sorry, man." Gage didn't add the *I told you so* Luc half expected to hear. "At dinner on Friday night when I saw you two together, I actually started believing you might make it work. That you were getting the do-over most people never have." Gage paused from cleanup and tapped against his chest. "Almost made this stone heart of mine pump with blood again."

Humor surfaced. While Gage had shut down since Nicole left, Luc was certain the man underneath all of that still existed. But it would take someone amazing to carve him back to life again.

"Cate found the paperwork. After I promised her I wouldn't file for custody and that we'd work things out." Luc bent to the ground, unhooking the trap shooter from the battery as another raindrop nailed his ear.

"Oh." Gage scraped a hand along the back of his hair. "Can't help feeling like that's my fault."

"It's not. I should have just told her about it. Or thrown it away. I tried explaining that I didn't plan to do anything with it, but she didn't believe me."

The churning clouds held Gage's attention. "I always believed Nicole. I was naive. Never thought she'd do any of the things she did." He collected shells, tossing them into the plastic trash bin. "Not to make it about me."

"I'd rather talk about you than me."

"So what are you going to do?" Gage snagged the other side of the thrower and they hoisted it into the back of the truck.

Luc slid it forward along with the other supplies and then slammed the tailgate shut. "Do? Nothing. Be a dad to Ruby. Try to move on."

"Aren't you going to go after her? Fight for your family?"

Now he sounded like Mackenzie. "Would you? Did you?" The questions came out harsher than Luc planned. But he was curious. Gage didn't talk a lot about what had happened between him and his ex-wife.

"The difference is, I didn't have anything left to fight for. Nicole was gone long before she actually took off. I was just holding on so tight, trying so hard to keep her, that I wouldn't let myself see the truth. But you, on the other hand…you do have something worth fighting for. Ruby. And the fact that you love her mother—because I'm guessing that's the case—is the best thing you could ever give her." Gage swiped at a raindrop that landed on his forehead. "I thank God every day that Nicole and I didn't have kids who would have to deal with our split."

Luc hadn't thought about it that way. He'd only been focused on loving Cate and her not returning the sentiment. But in all of Cate's desire to protect Ruby, she'd forgotten one thing—that their daughter would benefit from the three of them being a family. Ruby would be over the moon about it. What would make her feel safer than that?

"But Cate doesn't trust me. How do I handle that?"

"Why doesn't she?"

Luc was about to fill Gage in on what had happened between them in the past when understanding hit him like a left hook.

Her parents.

Each had pitted her against the other when she was just a little girl. They should have protected her. Instead, they'd destroyed her ability to trust.

It wasn't about him. It had never been about him.

"Her parents broke her heart, I think." And then he'd come along and done the same. Twice.

Cate struggled with believing him, but it wasn't because he was untrustworthy—though that was how she'd made him feel. It was because the very people who should have adored her had done the opposite. They'd been focused on themselves.

In Cate's world, love had to be earned. It wasn't freely given. She didn't believe that anyone could love her unconditionally. But Luc wanted to be the one to prove her theory wrong.

He already loved her that way. Just because she'd moved back to Denver with Ruby didn't mean he'd stopped. It had just been laced with hurt and confusion the past few days.

But now, thanks to Gage—and maybe with slight credit to Mackenzie—he knew exactly what he wanted. He just had to figure out how to get it.

"When are we going back to the ranch, Mommy?"

Six days of the same question from Ruby. Each time Cate answered in a high-fructose corn-syrup tone. Fake. Overly sweet. Trying for patience with everything in her.

"I'm not, sweetie. We're going to live here in our apartment, remember? But your dad's going to pick you up for a sleepover in a little bit. So you'll go to the ranch sometimes, when he has you."

"Why aren't you going?" Ruby's tiny brow crinkled with the innocent question.

"Because Mommy has work to do." Her favorite fallback. Cate should do something today besides work—go somewhere, be with friends. But she didn't have the energy. "You'll have a good time with your dad."

The one friend she had been communicating with—surprisingly enough—was Emma. Cate had received a text from her on Sunday night, a few hours after she and Ruby had left the ranch.

Just wanted to make sure you got home okay. We miss you both already.

Cate wasn't sure who the "we" referred to, but she was confident it wasn't Luc. Not after how things had ended between them. But Emma had been sweet to include Cate in that second part.

She'd responded, and they'd texted every day since.

Luc, on the other hand, had only contacted Cate once this week. He'd texted to tell her that he'd pick up Ruby this morning. That had been it. He hadn't even responded to the email she'd sent with logo options for the ranch.

The whole situation was eerily similar to the last time they'd fought.

During the week, Cate had gone over and over what Luc had said in his office on Sunday. But when the desire to believe his explanation surfaced, she snuffed it out.

She just…couldn't. Not when she'd seen the proof.

It was better to nip things between her and Luc now, before they got too out of hand. Before she was crushed beyond repair.

Oh, wait. Too late for that.

Cate had hoped they could salvage things for Ruby and prevent her from getting hurt, but that ship had also sailed. Ruby had really struggled this week, whining and crying at the slightest things.

So much for Cate's plan to keep her daughter safe. Unaffected. Protected and loved.

Ruby's lower lip protruded. "I want you to come."

"You don't need me, sweets. Your dad will take great care of you." The truth of those statements pricked like a needle. Luc was fantastic with Ruby. Especially for having come into fatherhood years into her little life. Cate might not be happy about what he'd done with the custody stuff, but she could give him that.

Right before leaving the ranch, Cate had given Luc a schedule of times for keeping Ruby. He'd said they worked for him, and that had been the last of it.

So far. But he could still choose to file

for custody. What reason did he have not to now?

"I don't want to go to Ms. Betty's house anymore, Mommy."

Cate swallowed the groan begging for escape. She didn't know what to do with this new Ruby. The girl had always adored day care. People. Anything new. But since they'd been back and she'd returned to Betty's on Tuesday, Ruby had been full of complaints and stomachaches. She'd tried every excuse to stay home: *My tongue feels silly. I can't find my bear. The horses at the ranch need me.*

So far Cate had been conveniently blaming Luc for Ruby's angst. If he hadn't convinced them to live at the ranch, Ruby wouldn't know that other life existed. She wouldn't have fallen in love with the freedom, the place and the people.

"Let's not think about Ms. Betty's today. You have two days off."

Luc was planning to keep Ruby until after

church on Sunday. At that point they'd meet up to exchange her.

A knock sounded at the door, and Cate checked the peephole. Luc. Already? Thankfully, she'd changed out of pajamas and into a light blue T-shirt and capris this morning. She opened it. "Hey, you're—"

"Early. I know." He didn't even have the decency to look chagrined. Luc strode into the living room as Cate's mouth fell open. She hadn't even invited him in! He could go wait in his truck.

Only…he had insisted on driving all the way here to pick up Ruby. And he hadn't fussed about the schedule she'd suggested. She should probably count those as victories and not stick a broom handle into a hornet's nest.

The door slipped from her fingertips, closing just as Ruby flew into Luc's arms, their embrace reminiscent of years of separation.

"I missed you this week, Rube-i-cube."

"I miss-ded you, too, Daddy."

Cate blinked away moisture. Now was not the time to break down.

Luc lowered Ruby to the carpet. "Why don't you grab your stuff, okay?"

"Okay!" She took off for her room.

Sitting on the couch, Luc stretched long legs in front of him, acting like he owned the place. "So, Cate, how've you been?"

"Fine." The word snapped out, nowhere near the truth.

"Good for you. How have I been? So nice of you to ask. Not fine, actually." She couldn't decipher the message that radiated from his stormy eyes. "Here." He shifted to retrieve something from his back pocket. Held a white envelope toward her.

Cate's knees swirled, fear stirring her emotions into a tornado-like spin. What was in the envelope? Was he planning to file and telling her up front?

Please no. Ruby deserves better from us. God, I'm begging. They might have to share her, but they didn't have to fight over her.

"What…what is that?"

"Something from Gage."

Gage? That didn't give her peace of mind. She took it but made no move to open it.

Luc stood and crossed over to her, stopping only when he'd invaded her personal space. Fresh-air scent clung to his clothes, and Cate resisted swaying closer to breathe him in.

She'd missed him this week. The thought came without permission. When would she get a handle on the emotions Luc had reignited in her over the past month?

"You really don't believe me, do you? Do you think that's about custody?" He pointed to the envelope.

She looked to the floor, attempting to hide the truth, but her resolve weakened. "Yes." She wanted to scream it, distress bubbling to the surface.

"It's not." Luc's hands fisted. "I said it on Sunday and I'll say it again. I love you, Cate." His voice had dropped low, probably so that Ruby wouldn't hear, but the effect registered even stronger. Her bones reverberated with the intensity. "I was never going to file for custody. I agreed to your dates. They work for me, so I'm still not going to. You asked me not to battle over Ruby, and I plan to honor that."

He edged closer, and even though Cate wanted to step back, she didn't. Part of her was drawn to him. Unable to move.

"Last time I fought with you, not for you. And I'm not going to make that mistake again." His finger bounced between them. "We're nowhere near through, just so you know."

Could a person's lungs deflate from sheer shock? Because hers were no longer functioning.

"I don't know what it's going to take to prove that I love you and that I'm never going to stop. When we were younger, I let anger win. Not this time. I want the three of us to be a family, and I'm going to keep fighting for you. For us. Until you know you can trust me. Because you can."

"I'm ready, Daddy!" Ruby bounded out into the living room, and Luc took a step back. Still wasn't enough space to calm Cate's ricocheting nerves, but she'd take it.

Ruby listed through the things in her bag, but Cate's mind was spinning too fast to manage a coherent thought. Plus, she'd already packed Ruby's stuff for her. So as long as she wasn't removing things, it should be fine.

"Sounds perfect, sweets." Her voice came out surprisingly even.

"Don't forget Boo-boo bear," Luc added, and Ruby disappeared down the hallway and into her bedroom.

"Then what's in this?" Cate held up the envelope.

"Gage's testimony. About what I said when he dropped off the papers. That I never planned to do anything with them. I thought it might help if you had someone to back my side of the story."

Cate needed time to process. To deal with everything Luc was throwing at her.

"Got him! Boo-boo was sad I almost left him, but I gave him a smooch and made it all better." Ruby's arms wrapped around Cate's legs. "I love you, Mommy." Her sadness from earlier had been replaced with excitement, and Cate wasn't going to ruin that for her. She caught her daughter in a big hug and said goodbye.

As Luc pulled the door shut behind them, his hazel eyes held hers until the last second, saying everything she wanted to hear but fought believing.

At the click of the knob, she dropped onto the sofa, head falling into her hands, and did the only thing she knew to do.

She prayed.

Chapter Sixteen

"I'm so glad you called." Emma slid into the booth across from Cate at the small café located about halfway between the ranch and Cate's apartment.

"Really? I keep thinking you're going to cut me off because Luc and I…" Cate wasn't sure exactly how to finish that sentence. Fought? Couldn't get on the same page?

It was more that she couldn't trust him. Anyone, for that matter.

"Nah. If I had to pick between the two of you, I'd probably choose you."

Cate laughed, appreciating the sentiment

even while knowing how loyal Emma was to her family.

"Now, Mackenzie, on the other hand…" Emma sprouted a cheeky grin. "Would you believe she's come around to your side?"

What? Impossible. Mackenzie was Team Luc all the way. "How did that happen?"

"She got to know you. We all did. And she's just as annoyed at our brother for doing something stupid to mess things up between you guys. Before you left, we thought you and Luc were getting back together and we were both happy for you. Well, I was ecstatic. Mackenzie was cautiously optimistic." Amusement lit her face but quickly fell. "It had felt…right."

It had felt right. Until it had gone so wrong. Again.

"Do you two even know what happened?"

"Not the details. Luc's been pretty tight-lipped."

"And you're still taking my side?"

"I'm on both of your sides. I want what's

best for all three of you. You're family, too, Cate. You're my niece's mom. That counts. Plus, my friend."

Just like that, Cate's tight nerves began to ease. Emma, as usual, was good medicine.

This morning after Luc left, Cate had been a mess. She'd prayed and cried and read her Bible. Last time when she and Luc broke up, she'd barely been more than a kid, and she'd had no relationship with God. This time, no matter how confused she was, she had someone to turn to. Eventually, she'd left her apartment with peace. No answers, but confident that God would guide her. Maybe even with a kick in the pants. Cate needed those nudges more than she liked to admit.

The waitress approached and took their drink orders.

After she left, Cate leaned forward, resting her arms on the table. "It's not all his fault, you know." It was and it wasn't. Why'd Luc have to ask about custody paperwork in the first place? But then again, wouldn't she have done the same in his shoes? She had kept his daughter from him for over three and a half years.

Luc had said he wasn't going to follow through on filing. And Cate had no doubt he was upset she hadn't believed him. Again. But it was *so hard* for her to trust.

"He denies doing what I think he did." Or planned to do in the future. Cate wasn't sure how much more to tell.

Emma's soda and Cate's iced tea arrived at the table. The younger girl took a sip through her straw, face contemplative. "If there's one thing I can say about Luc, it's that he's honest. He might not always be the most patient, and he's definitely made his share of mistakes in life, but he always tells the truth. It's just part of who he is. He can't help it."

Emma opened and studied her menu as if her comments hadn't just leveled Cate to the ground.

When Luc had explained how the paperwork had ended up on his desk, Cate had thought it made sense. That the story rang true. But she'd held on to distrust instead of choosing to believe him. She'd latched on to the papers in front of her instead of the man standing inches from her.

The unopened envelope from Gage was in Cate's purse. She hadn't broken the seal... because she didn't want to read it and find out Luc was telling the truth. Where would that leave her? Ripped wide open. He'd been her first love, but now he was her second, too. Their relationship was different this time around. They did a lot less fighting. A lot more talking. Luc had coaxed so many things out of her. He made her feel loved. Safe. The month with him had brought back to life the feelings lying dormant inside her.

And that was scary stuff.

If she believed Luc, that meant she'd have to tell him how she felt. That she loved him and didn't want to live without him in her life or Ruby's. That she wanted the three of them to be a family, too.

Cate had been searching for something she'd never find—assurance that she and Luc wouldn't turn out like her parents. But life didn't work that way. She wasn't going to know what was around the next bend. Just what stood in front of her. And a few hours ago, that had been Luc.

Thinking of him, standing in his office and her living room, confessing his feelings to her while she didn't accept them…didn't even acknowledge them. Her face heated. She'd been so awful to him. What had she done?

Cate knew Emma's words were true—she could trust Luc. Not only that, for the first time, she wanted to.

God had heard her desperate prayers for wisdom and guidance earlier today, and He'd softened her, making fear dissipate while faith took its place.

And with a little unintentional nudge from

Emma, Cate could finally admit she loved Luc. It was frightening to think it. Would be even harder to say it. But it was the truth.

Giddiness swam through her torso, warming her face. Good thing Emma still studied the menu, because Cate's features were surely displaying her every thought. Not that Emma would mind the change.

"Do you know what you're going to order?" Wrinkles marred Emma's usually smooth forehead—the only part of her visible behind the massive menu.

"Luc." Cate slapped a hand over her mouth and consequent burst of laughter.

The menu lowered, steel blue eyes sparkling with merriment over the top. "I think that's a good choice for you. Though I won't say that I'm going to have the same."

Luc sat on the floor next to Ruby's twin bed, his back against the small side table.

"Daddy." She shifted to face him, head

creating a small indent in her pillow. "Is Mommy going to say good-night to me?"

And there went his heart. Trampled to pieces all over again. How many times could the thing take a beating and get back up?

"She's not staying at the ranch tonight, remember? You'll see her tomorrow." Things had gone well since Luc had picked up Ruby this morning, but nighttime was proving to be tough.

He hated that this was the normal they had to adjust to. It wouldn't be if Luc had anything to say about it. But his conversation with Cate this morning had been stilted, and Luc wasn't confident that he'd gotten through to her.

All day he'd been praying. Begging God that Cate would come around. And he'd been asking for peace for Ruby. So far he wasn't sure any of his requests were making a hill of beans difference.

"I miss Mommy."

"I do, too." Oops. He hadn't meant to admit that.

Ruby giggled. "You're silly, Daddy."

He crossed his eyes and stuck out his tongue, earning another laugh.

Tonight they'd gone into town and had ice cream. Then Ruby had played at the park while Luc had sat on the bench alone. Missing Cate. Missing what he'd so recently hoped they could have.

"Will you read me one more book?"

How could he refuse that request? "Sure. Pick one out."

Ruby popped down from the bed, showing little sign of being tired, and dug through the small basket that held a few toys and books.

Emma and Mackenzie had shown up at his cabin earlier today with new pink sheets for Ruby's bed and the contents now spilling from the bin. Luc would never have thought of the small touches until too late. His sisters had saved the day. Ruby had noticed the stuffed bunny, brightly colored books and smattering of toys right away and been delighted by the finds.

"This one." She slid back under the covers.

Luc read *The Story of Ferdinand*—a bull who preferred to smell flowers over fighting. Which, pathetically, only reminded him of Cate, because: flowers.

"Your dad's a real sap, Rubes."

She patted him lightly on the cheek. "Good boy."

He closed the book and said a bedtime prayer, then pushed up from the floor, body complaining.

"I'll be right out here in the living room." He paused in her doorway. "I'll leave the door open, okay?"

She nodded, but the lurking sadness in her eyes slayed him.

Luc dropped onto the sofa, elbows on his knees, head in his hands. He hadn't realized how hard this would be—on Ruby, or on him. Though right now he was far more concerned about her.

Should he call Cate? Have her talk to Ruby? He wanted their daughter to feel safe and happy, not worried and anxious. Luc could ask Emma for help. She'd know what to do. But he didn't want to talk to his sister right now. The woman he wanted to communicate with had blocked him out of her life, and he wasn't sure how to worm his way back in.

Cate might not want to hear from him, but if it was about Ruby, he had the right to call, didn't he?

Before he could overthink anymore, he snagged his phone from the coffee table, found Cate's number and pressed Send. Just hearing her voice would be worth it. And she'd never be bothered about a phone call over Ruby. If there was one constant about Cate, it was the way she loved their daughter. If only that sentiment could be transferred over to him also.

"Luc?" His name held a multitude of questions and concern, so he answered before she could tumble down the mama-bear slope.

"Ruby's fine."

"Oh, good." Her relief practically oozed through the phone in his hand. A beat of silence stretched, and he pictured Cate refilling her lungs. Tense shoulders lowering. The woman was over-the-top protective of Ruby. Like one of those news stories about a mother lifting a car off her child—Cate could manage that with her pinkie finger if any harm came Ruby's way. "So what's up?"

"Ruby misses you. I did my best with her, but I'm just not sure it's enough. When we did the campout, I think she was comforted because you were minutes away and I could bring her home to you at any time. But now I think she's just overwhelmed by the changes." Luc could sympathize with that. He didn't like them, either. He would much rather be back to sleeping in the spare bedroom at the house and have Cate here. Or, even better, be able to call Cate his wife and all live in the same place.

"My reception isn't perfect, but I caught most of that. Do you need me to come?"

How should he answer? If it was up to him, yes. He wanted her here—for him and for Ruby. But he didn't want to disrupt her night alone, either. Maybe she had plans.

"I don't know," he answered honestly.

"Lucas." The sound of his full name warmed him. "I prayed a ton this week about Ruby staying at the ranch with you." He pieced her words together through the spotty reception. Where was she? Not at her apartment, if he had to guess. "And I really think God is going to work it out. Ruby's going to be just fine, whether I come or not."

Tension fled his body with Cate's encouragement. She was right. Ruby would be okay either way.

"Is it just Ruby who needs me?" Cate's

question was so quiet, he almost missed it. And then Luc was certain he'd misheard. How could she even ask something like that?

He needed Cate like oxygen. Or land under his boots.

Catherine Malory, if I tell you I love you one more time and you don't accept it as the truth, I'm going to lose my ever-loving mind.

A knock sounded on his door. Faint, but noticeable.

"Hang on a sec." Luc was thankful for the interruption. The time to know how to answer her if he had heard right. Because he didn't think yelling his thoughts from a moment ago would be the best option.

He swung the front door open to find Cate on the step. His hand—the phone still in it— slid down to his hip.

"What are you doing here? How did you get here so fast?"

She wore jeans that hugged her legs and brown leather sandals. A white shirt with dainty polka dots. Her hair framed her face and bright, vulnerable eyes that shone in the outside cabin light. The sight of her stole the moisture from Luc's mouth.

One shoulder lifted. "I was already on the way."

Bird wings fought for release from the confines of his chest. "To see Ruby?"

"No." A timid smile claimed her lips. "To see you."

Shock gripped him. He stood there silent, a thousand thoughts flying through his mind at once.

"Can I come in?"

A nod would have to suffice since his voice had gone missing.

Cate walked to Ruby's bedroom as Luc latched the door. She disappeared inside for a few seconds, then returned to the couch and sat. "Ruby's asleep." She looked at him expectantly.

Again mute, he followed, sinking onto the sofa.

"Lucas, I'm so sorry I didn't believe you

about the custody papers. That I didn't trust you right away. I do now."

The calmly said statements detonated, creating a roaring in his head. What did that mean? She wasn't exactly confessing her love for him. Was it just about Ruby for her? About them getting along for their daughter's sake?

"What changed your mind? Did you read Gage's note?" His friend had been factual but convincing, backing up Luc's story.

"No." She dug into her purse, handing him the still-sealed envelope. "I didn't need to. I already knew the truth. I'd just been denying it. I had lunch with Emma today." Luc hadn't known they were planning to meet. "And she said some things I needed to hear. But mostly confirmed what I didn't want to admit. Because then I'd have to confess that I love you, and I could get hurt. So could Ruby."

Cate kept going as if she hadn't just said three words that rocked his whole world.

"Choosing us…it's messy. Our relationship doesn't come with guarantees. And that's scary for me. Especially with what I grew up witnessing. But I don't want to let my parents' decisions control me anymore. So I'm letting faith win. I choose to believe you for—" she swallowed "—the rest of our lives, if you'll have me." She leaned forward, earnest. "Because, for Ruby's sake, we're either committed forever or nothing at all. I won't do that to her. And if you're not ready for that, that's okay. But those are my terms."

If he'd have her? *If?*

Those big, beautiful eyes of hers stared into his as her fingers squeezed his arm. "Lucas, can you forgive me for not believing you?"

"Do you think you can trust me in the future?"

Strength and peace radiated from her. "Yes."

"There's your answer."

Luc tugged Cate closer. He couldn't find

the words he wanted—they'd all fled the moment he'd opened the door to find her standing there—so he kissed her. For all of the moments that had gone before and for the future. One he already impatiently couldn't wait for.

Cate's arms wound around his neck. Hearing she loved him back drowned Luc in contentment. In bliss. It was a tie with finding out about Ruby. And in a month and a half, he'd gone from not having either of them to having both.

Thank You, God.

Luc made himself pull away from her captivating lips, knowing that if he had his way, kissing Cate would be a full-time job. He didn't go far—their arms were still tangled up like a jumbled pile of extra electrical cords. Considering Luc never wanted to let go, the next few years could get awkward.

Cate's eyebrows shot up. "So? You never responded to everything I said."

That kiss wasn't enough of an answer for

her? Luc grinned, fighting the desire to meet her adorable, questioning mouth again. She'd offered him forever—all or nothing—and he definitely had an answer for that.

"If that was a proposal, I accept."

Epilogue

Catherine Wilder needed to find her husband. Pronto. She'd scoured the cabin and lodge for him when she returned from town twenty minutes ago but had yet to catch sight of his maple cropped hair and strong shoulders.

Ones that would need to stay sturdy for the news she was about to share with him.

The red barn loomed up, reaching for the clear, crisp Colorado sky. Last place she knew to check.

She stepped inside, letting her eyes adjust to less light and cinching her red winter jacket with a fur hood tight around her to battle the biting air.

A crash sounded, and she followed it through the barn to the storage area behind.

Luc wrestled a stack of sleds into submission, hanging them on hooks that had been ignored by whoever had used the plastic saucers last.

His movements were quick. Precise. Of course, Luc was overqualified to be organizing sleds, but she imagined he'd come by, seen the mess and gotten to work.

She liked that about him. She liked a lot of things about her husband.

Cate and Luc had married a month after she'd shown up at the ranch for the second time in a small ceremony at the little white church they attended. Ruby had switched to a local preschool, where she only attended mornings and spent the rest of her day tagging along with Luc, Cate or one of her aunts. Their girl was delighted by her new life, as was her mama.

Approaching behind Luc, Cate wrapped her arms around his middle. Taut stomach muscles greeted her when she squeezed.

"Hey." His hands covered hers, returning the hug as he glanced over his shoulder, eyes alight. Luc turned, switching so that she was wrapped up in his arms. Pretty much the best place to be in the whole wide world.

He kissed her hello. It was likely meant to be short and sweet. A greeting. But it quickly morphed into something more. Cate lost herself for a minute, just because she could, then inched back while remaining in his embrace.

"Stop distracting me. I have something to tell you."

Luc's nose wrinkled with disgust. "I don't like that command."

She laughed. Held his face in her hands. "Focus."

"That I can do, Mrs. Wilder."

Whenever he called her that—and it was a lot—her stomach leaped and danced and threw a party. If Cate had known she could be this happy, she would never have wasted all of those years without Luc in her life.

He wasn't the answer to all life's problems, and they still had off moments, but they always came back to each other with love and figured out whatever tried to mess with them. And it wasn't much. Mostly, the transition from single parenting to a family of three had gone better than she'd ever imagined.

A good thing, considering what she had to tell him.

"I had my doctor's appointment this morning."

Cate had been feeling off. More tired than normal. So she'd gone to the doctor, just to make sure everything was okay.

"How was it? What did Dr. Sanderson say?"

"He said I do have something going on." She was toying with him a bit, but she couldn't help having a little fun. After all, she'd been reeling from the news for the last hour.

"What's wrong?" Luc tucked her hair back, eyes full of concern. "Is it something we can fix? Is he giving you something to help?"

"He is. Prenatal vitamins." Cate still couldn't believe she was pregnant when they'd taken precautions to make sure that didn't happen immediately. She and Luc definitely wanted more kids, but they'd planned to wait a bit. Give everyone time to adjust.

So much for that.

She'd asked the doctor, *"Are there ever people precautions just don't work for?"* Because if that was anyone's story, it was hers and Luc's. She should have known better. Expected it even.

He'd replied, *"Sometimes. Mostly, I think God just laughs at us, thinking we're so in control down here. He likes to remind us that, ultimately, we're not."*

Cate was gathering that message loud and clear.

Luc had morphed into a statue. He blinked slowly, numerous times. "What did you say?"

"I said he wants me to take a specific kind of prenatal vitamin for the babies."

Cate tamped down on her still-in-shock smile begging for release. She'd walked around town in a daze after her appointment, coming to terms with Dr. Sanderson's revelation that they were having twins.

The doctor had tried to determine how far along Cate was based on her cycle, but she'd been quite distracted lately and unable to fill in the dates he'd requested. Next thing she knew, he'd had her prepped for an ultrasound. Turned out, Dr. Sanderson did all of the health care in this town, from pregnant mama to the elderly. And lo and behold, two sacs had been visible. Cate totally wanted to blame Luc and Mackenzie for the development, but Dr. Sanderson had pointed out that an increased likelihood for fraternal twins was only hereditary on the mother's side, and identical twins were purely from chance.

"But I thought we weren't…that couldn't… Did you say *babies*?" Luc put emphasis on the *s*.

"That's what I thought, too. And yes, as in plural. Twins."

His head shook, eyes crinkling and shining with moisture. And then he laughed, elation spilling from him. Cate had known it would be okay—that Luc would be supportive, possibly even excited. But she hadn't expected this reaction.

Suddenly, her feet flew off the ground. Luc had swept her up in a hug and now swung her around in a circle. "You are amazing." He let her down slowly, her lined winter boots meeting solid ground.

She wasn't sure why she deserved the credit for getting pregnant whenever Luc so much as glanced in her direction, but she chuckled at his boy-like delight. As if suddenly realizing the babies were already there with them, Luc reverently touched her stomach. He knelt and began talking to them.

He told them how much he loved their mother. Moisture filled her eyes. How much he loved their sister. One tear slipped free, quickly followed by more. And then he told them they were all going to be together. Forever.

A small hiccup escaped.

Luc rose to his full height, tenderness in his touch as he thumbed moisture from her cheeks. "What's wrong? Why are you crying?"

"I don't know." But she knew pieces of it. "How are we going to handle two babies at once? And where will we live? And—"

"My sisters already offered us the house and we refused. Now we accept. They'll take the cabin and be perfectly fine. And there's two of us. Plus Emma and Mackenzie. You'll have a village of help this time. You won't be on your own."

His words should have induced guilt, but they didn't anymore. Luc had forgiven her so completely for not telling him about Ruby that there wasn't even a hint of malice in his statement. Cate had never experienced such a deep, abiding, freely given love from another human before. Not dependent on her behavior. Because if it was, she wouldn't be standing here face-to-face with the man she loved.

"You're right." She motioned to her cheeks and the flash of tears that had now ceased. "When I found out, I may have panicked. Just a touch."

His grin eased into play. "I think that's understandable. I'm sorry I didn't go with you to the appointment. I should have." He drew her close, holding her snug against his chest. "We're going to be just fine, Mrs. Wilder."

"I love you, Lucas." The declaration was

muffled by his jacket, but she knew he'd heard by the tight squeeze that followed.

He pulled back enough for their gazes to meet. "I love you, too." A gentle kiss landed on her forehead. "So much that I'm not sure how I ever survived without you." The emotion of his statement coupled with what was to come, the wide-open future, the unexpected gift of more *babies*, all with this man...it crashed into her, almost making her sway.

Thankfully, Luc held her steady. Just like he always did.

* * * * *

If you enjoyed this story,
pick up these other books by Jill Lynn:

FALLING FOR TEXAS
HER TEXAS FAMILY
HER TEXAS COWBOY

Available now from Love Inspired!

Find more great reads at
www.LoveInspired.com

Dear Reader,

When I was on a walk in our neighborhood, I reached a house where the mom and little girl were outside. In the thirty or so steps it took me to pass their home, she greeted me, asked numerous questions and jabbered the whole time. She was outgoing and bright and adorable, and in that moment, the character of Ruby was inspired. Sometimes it's just a little spark that gives an idea wings.

This book has been helped along by so many. Thank you to Lost Valley Ranch in Colorado for your incredible help and beautiful guest-ranch setting. Thank you to my sister, brother-in-law and niece, who let me use pieces of their story as inspiration for Luc's and Ruby's special hearts. And to my readers—thank you for all of your input and contributions to this book. I couldn't do it without you all, and truly, it's so much more fun with you. You are, quite simply, the best.

If you're not hanging out on my Facebook

or Instagram pages, I hope you'll come over and join us. (@JillLynnAuthor for both.) For upcoming book releases and sales, sign up for my newsletter at Jill-Lynn.com/news.

Jill Lynn